UNRELIABLE BEHAVIOUR

Derek Walsh

Raider Publishing International

New York   London   Cape Town

Cover Images Courtesy of iStockPhoto.com

ISBN: 978-1-61667-288-1

Published By Raider Publishing International
www.RaiderPublishing.com
New York London Cape Town
Printed in the United States of America and the United Kingdom

To Ciaráin and Jon Squash – my dear friends always.

A special thanks to Michael Sszenkuma, Paul Allen, Rachel, Diana and Peter, Warwick and my family and friends.

UNRELIABLE BEHAVIOUR

Derek Walsh

1

Miles Goodwin

Miles sat expressionless as he slumped into his sandwich-encrusted and coffee-stained seat on the 12:27 to Euston. "Oh my God. What the fuck have I done?" he screeched rather loudly, furtively looking around to see if anyone had noticed his outburst.

After all, anyone sitting by themselves who speaks under their breath and is heard by others, is, at best, seen as eccentric and, at worst, someone who may be prone to carrying knives; big knives, pointy knives. However, if that same person *shouts* out a question, he may be prone to using that knife. Fortunately, no one had noticed this outburst. There were only two other people in his carriage; one was an elderly nun who appeared to be smiling aimlessly into space. No doubt her mind was focussed on thoughts of a more celestial nature. The second was the most clichéd-looking backpacker imaginable. You know the type. Full beard; massive backpack fully adorned with the badges of all the various countries he'd supposedly visited. Straight out of lonely planet travellers' guide. He was either completely stoned or pissed, or perhaps both, so it was unlikely he'd heard anything.

Miles never really understood what his mum had seen in Craig. *Yeah*, he thought, *he's good looking if you like the no-nonsense, rugged type. But he's mean and crude, and*

Mum could have done a lot better. She's an educated woman who has won prizes for short story competitions and *she's second choice organist for St. Mary's.*

Miles remembered Dad taking them all out to the Roman Wall every Sunday after church. When they got home afterwards, they'd all sit down to Sunday lunch. And the way Dad looked at Mum used to embarrass Miles as a kid. Now, he couldn't think of anything more he'd rather see. After Dad died, Mum went to pieces. Before Dad died, all Miles' mates used to piss him off by saying that they thought his mum was fit. He used to lose it with them, but, deep down, he loved it. It made him proud, in a way. After Dad's death, Mum stopped caring. Shortly after that, she met Craig, that silver-tongued Irish wanker.

He stuck his head as far out the window as he could in order to say his final goodbyes to Carlisle. It was raining. In the distance, he could just about make out the imposing Dixon Chimney. He had hated it for as long as could remember in his short life, but, right now, he could feel an almost overwhelming need surge through his body to just to walk up to it, face it and touch it. He sat back in his seat awkwardly, stubbornly fighting back any tears that dared run down his face. *I'm a hard Cumbrian,* he thought, *and besides, I'm on me way to the smoke!*

In an attempt to somehow bring about a sense of normality and calm, he started to remove a number of items designed to alleviate the boredom of what was going to be a very long journey from his florescent backpack. First out came a soggy, half-eaten egg-mayonnaise sandwich that he'd bought from that grimy sandwich shop in the station, and a can of coke. Finally, out came his varied collection of magazines.

He had worked out that the stretch between Carlisle and Crewe was most likely going to be boring, except, of course, if you liked looking at sheep and the odd chimney.

Therefore, it was important to have the correct reading material to help alleviate this boredom. Boredom really wasn't an option. He needed to fully occupy his mind in order to escape from the terrifying thoughts presently occupying it. It may well turn out to be a futile gesture, but he didn't have the luxury to not try, at least. Paranoia was tightening its grip. He was consumed. He turned the pages of his magazine frantically in an effort to lose himself in its contents, but this was proving to be very difficult. His hands were becoming clammy. Each time he turned the pages, he left behind a fresh wet mark.

Ah man, this is no good. I just can't relax. I wish I hadn't done that. It was stupid. Really stupid. I'm too young to go to prison and everyone says I'm soft as shite. I'll end being someone's bitch. I've really screwed it up. I wish Mum was here. He was now beginning to descend deeper and deeper into a dark world of panic. *I've got to get me head together, or I'll blow it. The journey will end before it's even had a chance to begin.*

He continued to flick through the pages in a further frantic attempt to disappear into his, by now, sweat-tainted sports magazine. The train had now pulled out of Warrington and, looking around, he noticed that the initial three inhabitants had swelled to around twenty. He didn't want it to get too full, because then he might be confronted with the possibility of having to share his table or the surrounding seats. Miles was like that; he liked his own space, but, when it suited him, he liked being the centre of attention.

He had undergone the types of personality tests in school, which are supposedly designed to determine which area of employment one should consider. Miles' test had shown him to be a *passive aggressive*. He wasn't really sure what the term meant. Well, he knew what passive meant and he also knew what aggressive meant, but he didn't think you could be both, because that just wouldn't make sense. Two opposite ends of the emotional spectrum together, unlikely. *Must have been a mistake. Had to be.* Mrs. Meacher, his career guidance tutor, had been 'unable at present' to give a full explanation as to exactly what the term meant, as she was 'very busy and had others to assess'. In fact, apart from uttering the word 'nutter' under her breath as she had left the classroom, the subject was never really broached. However, Miles just put what he had had heard, or supposedly heard, down to his own paranoia and decided that he hadn't, in fact, heard anything. Miles was paranoid; everybody knew that, even the teachers.

The nun was no longer on the train. To his surprise, he was slightly disappointed. He wasn't religious, except perhaps on a Sunday when his parents whisked him off to church. For that half hour standing shoulder to shoulder with his fellow Sunday clubbers, as he called them, he felt cleansed of all wrong doing, pure as the proverbial snow. He really could have done with the sympathetic ear that he was told nuns were famed for. Although not born a Roman Catholic, he was aware that nuns, along with priests, had to adhere to a vow of confidence. After confessing his crime, not only would the guilt be lifted, she would also, upon hearing the contrite remorse in his little voice, have to give him absolution, leaving him with only one remaining worry, that of the threat of jail hanging over him. However, he'd missed his chance. He also noticed that the hippy had left. Miles wasn't overly fond of hippies. Perhaps that was Craig's malignant influence. He certainly wouldn't choose to take on any of Craig's opinions. He hated him. However, there was something about hippies that struck a chord with him. He couldn't quite put his finger on it. They just looked stupid and pointless to him. They looked daft and they appeared to be proud to look daft. Hippies, to Miles, were a pointless waste of time, and were there to be laughed at and ridiculed. He didn't hate them. He pitied them.

There were now a lot more people aboard the train for Miles to cast his all-knowing eye upon. Staring at him from the table opposite was a man in his fifties. He was dressed in the kind of trousers your uncle would wear; only he'd call them slacks. These nicely ironed slacks were then complemented with a plain white shirt and wine tank top. At a guess, he was probably a civil servant of some sort, although he could be a store manager at somewhere like WHS Smiths. Miles was feeling uneasy; he wondered why the man had his eyes fixed on him and didn't at all look like averting his gaze. It was more likely that he was looking past him and just happened to be looking in his direction. Even still, he was convinced that he was being stared at. He didn't like being stared at in the best of times, but he was on his own now and beginning to feel a bit vulnerable. Then, suddenly, a terrifying thought entered his head. *What if he's a copper? And, what if he's heard about me and knows what I've done? What if he's stalking me and letting me think I've got away with it, only to arrest me when I reach London?*

There comes a time in every man's life when he refuses to be scared any longer. The pros and cons of being timid and scared are weighed up and the conclusion drawn that situations will now be faced and the consequences of these actions accepted, even embraced. That person has become so tired of being afraid that he will ride bravely into battle on his wholly undernourished and inadequately sized steed. He will confront his windmills head on and, when he has defeated them, he will come back to make sure that they stay defeated. That they stay dead. He is on a mission. After a while, the windmills will reappear and the sequence of events will be repeated until he decides to take them on again and exact his bloody revenge. However, Miles isn't a man; he's still a boy.

The bastard, the fucking bastard. His emotions quickly turned from that of a scared young boy on a train to an irate teenager on his way to London. *If that wanker tries to grab me, I'll be away like shit off a stick and he'll have a heart attack before he gets anywhere near me, the crusty old git.*

Turning around and sticking his head slowly, but barely over the top, of his seat in order not to be seen, he noticed that there was a table full of business types. It was obvious they were all in good spirits and enjoying the journey. This was borne out by the fact that, every time the oldest businessman told a joke, the younger ones would all laugh at it. Then look out the window. However, it wasn't normal laugher; it was weird. The older man would tell the joke, then the not so older ones – as far as Miles was concerned, if you were over sixteen, you were cool, but if you were over twenty, you were old – would laugh in a way that made it look like a competition to see who could laugh the longest. *Very strange behaviour, indeed,* he thought. He also noticed that there were quite a few empty beer cans on the table, which probably went some way towards explaining this weird behaviour. *The lucky bastards,* he thought. *I wish I could be old every time I wanted beer, but young the rest of the time. Hang on, that man in the shop reached up and got FHM down off the shelf for me because I couldn't reach. Perhaps I can do no wrong? Maybe I'm on a roll and the barman will serve me beer!*

One of the first things Miles had done after boarding the train was use the toilet. When he had come out, he had noticed that the buffet car was close by. He felt better not having to ask anyone directions, as he was paranoid he might be clocked for who he was – a little upstart trying to get served alcohol. He made his way towards the buffet car, passing the empty palatial – when compared with his present seating arrangements – carriages of first class. *After I get me beer,* he thought, maintaining his positive mindset, *I'm going to travel first class. I've been on this train for nearly two hours and I've yet to see a ticket inspector. If there was one, he'd have been by now.*

Miles' heartbeat was beginning to increase in both rapidity and velocity the closer he got to the drinks hatches. *Perhaps this isn't a good idea, after all,* he thought. *What if the bloke who's serving doesn't serve me and reports me to whoever's in charge? Then that person asks me awkward questions like what is a sixteen year old doing travelling by himself.* And *what if the bloke in charge has been informed that I'm a runaway* and *he knows what I've done?*

The train was now pulling into a station; Miles looked out the window and could see that it was approaching Crewe. There were a lot of people standing on the platform. He decided that he would wait until people boarded the train. Then, if there were a few people who wanted to make a purchase, he would conceal himself among them, order his beer, then stick out his hand. Once to hand over the cash and again to receive his purchase. Amongst all that lot, he wouldn't be seen and the person serving would just be far too busy serving everyone; he wouldn't care. He wouldn't notice; far too busy to notice a little runaway like Miles. He had decided that, if he managed to pull this off, this story would be recounted to everyone who was willing to listen, except, of course, to his mum, Craig and the police.

Miles was no stranger to the delights of alcohol. Every weekend, he'd go around to Mark Saunders's place and Mark's older brother, Jamie, would get them a takeout. He was even allowed to stay over. By the time Mark's parents got back from the pub, they themselves were always too drunk to notice that their fifteen-year-old and his friend were in an even more enhanced state of inebriation than themselves. The next morning, Miles would be showered and fed a huge Mrs. Saunders fry up, which meant that, by the time he returned home, he was his mum's bright-eyed, tee-total boy. Again. Despite his fondness for this alcohol-induced hedonism, he always limited it to the weekend. Miles was sensible like that.

The train ground to a halt, sending him hurtling back towards first class sooner than he had planned. Getting back up and picking up his holdall, he quickly composed himself. To his delight, about ten of the people who boarded the train started to make their way towards the drinks hatch. "This is it, man," he said under his breath, in a lame attempt to spur himself on. "This is what you've been building up to."

Miles calmly walked up to the assembled group and quickly wedged himself in between a rather rotund, frumpy forty-something woman and her slightly slimmer and not so frumpy friend.

"Mind out there son," exclaimed the fatter of the two. "You'll do yourself an injury."

"Sorry Miss," said Miles coyly. "I should watch where I'm going, I really should." He played the sympathy card with flair.

"Listen, Pet," said the thinner of the two. "There's no point you trying to get served here."

Oh, that's it, thought Miles. *She's sussed me.*

"I mean, how are they supposed to see you?" she pointed out. "I tell you what, they'll have no such trouble where I'm concerned." She chuckled in a way only fat women do. "What if I get whatever you're after? That way, you won't have to keep jumping up and down, and the bar staff won't go out their minds just hearing voices."

"Are you sure?" enquired Miles. "You really don't mind?"

"Of course she doesn't mind," the fatter women interjected. "She'd hardly have asked otherwise, would she?"

Spurred on by this momentum, Miles decided to make his pitch. "All right then, I'd like four packets of crisps, salt and vinegar or beef, it doesn't really matter, a lion bar, or fruit and nut if they don't have a lion bar, and, yeah, erm, four cans of Stella. Actually, I can't remember if Jonathan wanted Strongbow or if Ciaráin wanted John Smiths. No that's it. We all want Stella. That's it. Stella for everyone. Stella all around. Four cans, please."

Then, for what seemed like an eternity of silence, Miles stood there motionless in anticipation. He slowly arched his head upwards to see if he could read her thoughts. To his dismay, she wasn't even looking at him.

Ah yeah, that's it I've done it now. I had to go and mess everything up, didn't I? And for what? A few cans of Stella? I really had to play the big man, didn't I? I've fucked it up. She's sussed me and she'll go up to the barman and whisper something in his ear. Then he'll go to a part of the bar where no one can see him, the part where the phone is, then call the police. After that, they'll find me and take me down to the station and fire questions at me. Then it'll all come out, like why I'm on me own on this train and why I left Carlisle. Maybe the police already know. I bet they've already been given a description. Ah, why did I do this?

Suddenly, from what seemed like miles above, came the long-awaited reply. "Sorry, lad."

This is it, thought Miles, his heart pounding.

"You seem to be out of luck, I can't see any Stella, but they've got Export. I know it's not the same, but it's better than nought. As for the crisps, you're totally out of luck; they're all gone. But they do have lion bars, so it's not all bad."

In a matter of seconds, Miles' feelings of dread suddenly turned to ones of quiet confidence. "Ah, don't worry, love." He had now decided to dispense with the word 'miss'. *After all, only kids call older lasses Miss,* he reaffirmed to himself. "Here's the money and have one for yourself," he offered as he handed over the sweat-soaked fifteen pounds that had been nestling in the palm of his hand all throughout this cliff hanger of an encounter.

"You're very kind," replied his new best friend. "You're a true gent."

Miles took the bag of delights in his hand and turned towards the corridor that contained first class – his new home for the next two and a half hours. "Set course for first class, me hearties," he mumbled in a swash, buckling type accent. "Aye, Cap'n." He pretended to be first mate. "First class it be."

He had decided that this was by far his biggest achievement to date. Nothing came close to this. Not even pulling Cynthia Jones on the school field trip to the Bolton Glass factory. Everyone had fancied Cyn, including Dennis Patterson, and *all* the girls fancied him, but Cyn didn't; she fancied Miles. Despite this amazing coup, it still didn't even come close to what had just happened. The first person he was going to recount this wonderful tale to was the person he was planning to stay with: Jez.

Jez was older than Miles by nearly three years. He was the typical bad boy. Parents – even his own – hated him and, more importantly, hated their sons – and daughters – having anything to do with him. By the time he was fifteen, he was known to practically every policeman in Carlisle; he was even on first-name terms with some of them. He was so familiar with the various police cells that he could even tell what station he was in, to the extent that, if someone named a piece of graffiti, he was able to pinpoint the police station it adorned. Parents may have hated him, but teenage lads hero worshiped him. If Jez spoke to you, you felt privileged. He was aware of his hero status among the kids, but never really got to know them on a one to one level, except, of course, Miles. That relationship had begun in haste when he had acted as lookout whilst Jez had relieved a small warehouse of its contents. Jez never forgot that and, as well as giving him twenty quid, he always said hello to him in front of all his mates, which, in the eyes of his mates, made him cool by association. Miles was now putting this favourable association to the ultimate test.

He was now standing outside the very first-class compartment that he had promised himself he would return to. It was still empty. In fact, all the first-class comparetments, bar one, were completely empty. *Has no one on this train got any money,* he joked to himself. *Bloody pikies, the lot of 'em.* "Remember, man," he muttered to himself, "there's no inspector; no bloody inspector; you're on a roll; nothing can stop you."

He pulled back the door and walked in. The first thing he noticed about his new surroundings was the smell. There was none. The other place smelt of stale sandwiches and bananas due to the fact that the bins were overflowing. It was also very untidy, and broken crisps lay scattered all around and under his table. However, this was first class; such shoddy standards would not be tolerated here.

He took his seat right by the window and placed his bag of delights on the table. To the right of the bag, he positioned his hold all in order to conceal its illegally acquired contents. Although he was on a roll, he didn't want to risk the possible chain of events that might be triggered if some do-gooder reported him for underage drinking. The culmination of which would involve him being taken away by the police for questioning relating to a certain incident in Carlisle.

He took the first can from the bag. His eyes lighted up. It was beautiful. It was refreshingly cold and covered in condensation. He was so happy. This was a moment worth savouring. He then began to wipe the condensation off to reveal all the lettering. There in plain English were the words, 'Carlsberg Export, brewed in Copenhagen by appointment to the royal court of Denmark, 5% by volume'. He looked closely again; he still wasn't ready to open it; he wanted to play with it a bit more.

He remembered seeing a wildlife documentary where a killer whale, having caught a seal, kept throwing it up in the air, then catching it in its mouth. This was repeated a number of times until the whale decided he was ready to eat the seal. For that moment, Miles was that whale. After an enjoyable time, tapping the can and bending back the ring, he decided that it was now time to consume his prey. He flicked open the can and brought it towards his face; he could feel the area surrounding his mouth get markedly colder the closer the can got. With the can touching his lips, he poured in its contents. "Oh my God," he gasped. "This is fucking top; the business; the bollox. It's lush!"

With the can now noticeably lighter, he contentedly placed it back on the table.

He let out a sigh, sat back into the seat and, with a look of contentment etched upon his innocent-looking face, looked out the window. It was raining again and the outside looked grey, but it was wild and anonymous, just like Miles. A tear trickled down his face. Not a tear to signify sadness, but one to signify pure contentment. He wiped it away and smiled; for the first time since leaving his house, he felt relaxed. There was no need to worry now; everything was going to be okay; everything was going to be just fine.

Now that his fears of getting rumbled could be dispensed with, he could get on with the business of deciding how long he was going to stay with Jez and what he would do once his money ran out. However, more importantly, he had to call his mum; otherwise, he would be constantly looking over his shoulder for the foreseeable future. Moreover, he had to call his mum, because he loved her and didn't want her to worry about him. Just because he hated Craig didn't mean he had to make his mum suffer. The possible consequences of his actions were now beginning to become clearer. Despite this, he knew that, if he was faced with the same situation, he'd do it all again.

In his new, somewhat calm frame of mind, he went through the series of events. He had just arrived home from Mark's. They had a history exam coming up the following Thursday and were brain storming together. Despite a premature taste for alcohol, both were very studious and hated doing badly at exams. Miles wanted to be an architect. Mark wanted to be a teacher. As soon as he had walked in through the door, he could hear shouting. Well, Craig had been doing all the shouting. He was a big man, with an 'action man' jaw and piercing blue eyes. Both Miles and his mum were scared of him; even the neighbours were scared of him. However, Miles seldom showed it. This was compounded by the fact that he had absolutely no respect for him and he made this blatantly obvious. Craig shouted to get his own way and it worked.

The shouting was coming from the kitchen. Miles went into the kitchen just in time to see Craig punch his mum. He was furious. If he had been capable of kicking Craig to death, slowly, he would have revelled in doing so. The look of hate on Miles' face had said it all and, for once, Craig appeared intimidated.

"And just what in God's name are ya going to do about this?" Craig had yelled.

Miles, despite being a paltry five point four inches short in comparison to Craig's large six point four frame, was no longer scared. He was furious.

"Touch me mum or me again and you'll find out, you fucking animal," came his defiant reply. "C'mon then; c'mon, you thick bastard."

Craig had then come towards Miles with his hands clenched. The fear factor had now returned to join Miles' all-consuming feelings of rage. In a move that had seemed like it was in slow motion, Craig had let fly. Miles had ducked; Craig had lost his balance and fallen against the fridge. Miles had then picked up the nearest thing to him, which was a wok, swung and hit Craig's head as hard as he possibly could.

Ironically, the wok had been a birthday present given to Craig by his brother the week before. Since receiving it, he'd used it practically every day and had been jokingly told by one of his mates that all this Chinese food would 'eventually kill him'!

Craig had just lain there motionless. Miles' mum had stood trembling in shock. He'd known he had to act quickly; he hadn't time to think. He had kissed his mum, told her he'd be in touch and walked calmly out the door. He had made his way to the train station, withdrew all his money, bar ten pounds, from his bank account, phoned Jez, and then bought a ticket to London. And, here he was now, two hours away from his destination.

He reached into his bag and took out his mobile phone. He turned it back on.

There were seven missed calls. *This doesn't look good,* he thought. The screen was showing good reception, so he had no excuse. His heart was racing. "I must compose myself; must compose myself," he said quietly.

He started pacing all around the compartment. There was no one else in this carriage, so he wouldn't have to worry about being overheard taking to himself. He opened another can of lager. "Right, Milesy, count to ten."

One, two... He got as far as four, then started to dial his mum's mobile. His mum knew he didn't like Craig, and had bought two phones, one for him and one for her. This meant they could conduct phone conversations free from Craig's interference.

"Miles, Miles, is that you, love, is that you?" his mum cried desperately.

Miles opened his mouth, but the words couldn't come out. He was suddenly overcome with all manner of emotions. He felt guilty because of the anxiety he now knew he had caused his mum. He also felt a strong sense of fear, because he still didn't know if he had killed Craig, and, to cap it all off, he felt a striking sense of loneliness upon hearing his mother's voice.

"Aye, it's me, Mum," came his reply; trying his best not to sound upset. "Mum, one question. One question. Please answer yes or no."

"No!" said his mum. "I know what you're going to ask and the answer's no, you haven't killed him. He's still alive. To be honest, when I saw you hit him as hard you did, with his own precious wok, I thought you had. It's just as well he's the overgrown brute that he is."

Miles sat back down, and disappeared into his deeply comfortable first-class seating. He could feel three hours of worry escaping from his person. He was sure his mum had heard.

"Oh my God," he exclaimed. "I can't tell you how relieved I am. So what happened after I twatted, sorry, Mum, hit him? Was he down for long? Did you have to call an ambulance? Oh, and, is he going to press charges?"

"Well, as you know, son, I was in shock," she explained. "All I could do was just look at him, and he wasn't moving; he was just lying there. I must've been looking at him for ten minutes before I called the ambulance."

"You didn't tell them what happened?" interrupted. Miles frantically.

"Of course not, pet," his mum answered reassuringly. "I told them he was doing a spot of DIY, fell off his step ladder and hit his head against the fridge. I even brought the ladder down from up stairs and laid it out in the kitchen. No one suspected a thing. After phoning the ambulance, I took his pulse. It seemed fine. He came to just as the ambulance was arriving. The first thing he did was apologise for hitting me. He didn't have any memories involving the wok or you, because, if he had, he would have mentioned it. When the ambulance came and they saw that Craig had regained consciousness, they insisted on carrying out a few tests on him, in order to make sure he was okay, and he was. So, are you going to come home now, love?"

A rather uneasy pause followed. "Look, Mum," said Miles, with a tinge of guilt in his voice. "I'm glad – well, relieved is a better word – Craig's not dead. I'm sorry for putting you through all this worry, but I can't stand living in the same place as that bastard. I'm sorry for saying that, Mum, but that's what he is. I hate the way he shouts at you all the time and the constant threats he makes to both of us. For whatever reason, I've made the break. If I hadn't left today, I would have left next week; it was only a matter of time. I'm not saying I won't come back to Carlisle again. I will, but I'm never coming back to live in the same place as that nutter. I have money and I'll be able to get some kind of work."

"But, pet," said his mum, with desperation in her voice.

"Look, Mum, I'll phone you every week and let you know how I'm getting on. I might even come back for Christmas."

"But Miles, I'll speak to Craig," his mum pleaded.

"Look, Mum," he continued, his voice beginning to break, "I'll be fine. I've got to go now. I'll phone you in a few days. I love you."

Before his mum could reply, Miles turned his phone off. It was better that way. If he had given his mum the chance to reply, the first thing he'd be doing once he arrived in London was buy a ticket back to Carlisle, and that wouldn't be good for anyone, not even Craig. The important thing was that Craig wasn't dead and the only thing he had to worry about at this present time was whether he'd be rumbled for sitting in a first-class carriage without the correct ticket. Hearing his mum's voice had also been a great source of comfort. He could now arrive in London without the unnecessary baggage of worry or guilt.

He smiled and relaxed into his seat again. The rain had stopped, but it was still a bit overcast. There were a lot of high buildings, which meant they were probably coming into Birmingham.

London was just over an hour away and he couldn't wait to get there. He and his mates had always talked about getting out of Carlisle and going to London or Birmingham. To Miles, Carlisle was his hometown and he was proud of it, but he always knew he'd end up in London. He just hadn't imagined it would be at such a young age and under such circumstances. He was, of course, going to miss Carlisle, especially going down Brunton Park to shout on United every other week. This, however, was insignificant, as he would now have to focus on a far bigger picture.

By now, he had consumed three cans of larger and half his Lion bar. Such was his excitement at procuring these beverages; he had managed to do this in under an hour. When he was at Saundie's place, they would consume four cans over a period of four hours and be legless at the end of it. So, three cans in under an hour was a personal best for him.

He looked out the window; it was raining again. This time, it was hitting the window in waves as opposed to drops of rain. It was as if the train was passing through a carwash for trains in the midst of its most intense cycle. Such was the intensity of this downpour, he could barely see the scenery outside. All he could make out were colours, mainly green and a bit of brown. He guessed they were probably passing through the countryside. He looked at his watch; it was 4:05 PM, which meant that he couldn't be more than half an hour from London.

For Miles, London had always been an enigma. 'The big smoke'; 'the main place' – these were the most common terms he used when referring to it. To him, it represented the best alternative to his home town. It was everything Carlisle wasn't. It was big, fast, exciting, happening, strange, cool, alive, pulsating, fascinating, engaging, enthralling, bold and full of surprises. He would make his mark here. This was where he would earn his spurs. It was where he would come of age. It was where the boy would become a man. Of course, London wasn't just about positives; it was also dirty, vile, cheap, disposable, dishonourable, harsh, angry and very unforgiving. It also housed its fair share of pimps, ponces, skag heads, slags, wideboys, dealers, dodgy dealers, gang leaders, bent coppers and crime bosses. Of course, Miles didn't need to concern himself with such mere details. He hadn't killed Craig, his mum still loved him and he had Jez in his corner.

He looked out the window again. It wasn't raining now. The buildings were definitely a lot taller. Not like skyscrapers, but Victorian townhouses complete with ground-floor pub and hanging basket. He was now approaching London. He gathered together his bundle of magazines and put them back in his bag. He looked at the table where four empty cans of lager stood. He was now ready to face his new world.

2

Jez

Miles stepped off the train. He was feeling slightly bewildered and uneasy. Here he was. Here he finally was. After all those years of yearning to go to the big smoke, he had finally fulfilled his dream. Though not in the manner in which he had intended. Due to the nature of his being here, and the sense of urgency he felt towards getting a base and getting settled, the impact of this realisation was somewhat diminished.

He looked around frantically in an attempt to spot Jez. Even if he had spotted him, he wasn't sure if he would recognise him. After all, three years in a teenager's life is a long time; in some cases, a mini lifetime. It's during that period in one's life that a metamorphosis takes place. This is a metamorphosis of physicality, whereby unwanted mini-red hills punctuated by a white tip on its summit appear on the face. These unwanted guests could at least have the decency to appear in less obvious places, places out of sight of the naked eye. This is, of course, only a transient unsightliness, however, as, once the moulding has been completed, the ugly duckling is transformed in to a gracious swan, though, sadly, not in all cases. Miles, unlike many of his peers who had fallen foul to the dreaded 'zit', was lucky in that respect. He was one of the anointed ones, the ones who would never fall victim to such outward blemishes, though he certainly had a few pronounced inner ones.

Suddenly, Vivaldi's haunting and poignantly harrowing 'winter' sauntered up towards the rafters of the mezzanine area. Miles rummaged around inside his sports bag and pulled out his phone.

"Welcome to the smoke country, boy! I trust your journey was a pleasant one," said Jez, attempting to affect a sophisticated London accent.

"Well," said Miles. "Apart from shitting meself most of the way down, I suppose you could say yes, it was rather pleasant. I'll tell ya all about it. Where are ya?"

"I'm on the other side of the ticket barrier. Just head towards the ramp and I'll see ya. I'll be the one insanely waving me hands around like a loon."

Miles continued up the ramp towards the barrier. Although he was meeting someone he knew and had the reassurance of a place to stay, he was, nonetheless, still feeling uneasy. He looked around him at all the people and the surroundings, and he was now really beginning to feel a bit overwhelmed by the whole experience. As he got closer, he could, as promised by Jez, see a tall, spiky haired, skinny man in his late teens waving his hands around like a complete lunatic. Miles smiled. He appreciated the comedic respite within the theatre of foreboding. Jez smiled back.

"Well, Miles, man, ya still look like the naïve little twat I remembered you to be. It's good to see ya, man, though I'd never imagined that I'd be seeing you here after you being forced to go on the run for attempted murder!"

Miles shook his head in a rather lame attempt to force a laugh, but, by now, he was so overwhelmed by the whole experience, he was close to tears. Jez could sense this, and immediately leant forward hugged him and patted him on the back.

"Haway, Miles, man," said a smiling Jez. "Let's get gan."

They started off towards one of the exits. Along the way, Miles was looking all around him, fascinated by the ostentatious station concourse. *Wow, all those different shops. Did the shops come first and the train station later? Or were the shops built in order to capitalise on an endless stream of customers?* He smiled smugly at this chicken and egg scenario.

They reached the exit. It was a dark, dusky autumn night with a slight chill. Miles looked around from side to side. *There seems to be an unending number of red double-decker busses and there are so many people. So many different types of people.* His feeling of foreboding was beginning to be joined with one of excitement. He smiled again, this time for slightly longer. Jez, noticing the slightly more upbeat refrain, shook his head and smiled back. "C'mon, you daft fucker."

They continued walking until they reached Euston Road. It was very busy and the traffic was at the obligatory rush-hour standstill. They continued walking across the road and in between the cars. Excitement was beginning to overtake Miles' feeling of foreboding and was now the prominent emotion showing on his face.

After another few minutes, and on passed a closed newspaper kiosk, and along what seemed like a somewhat deserted street, they came to what looked like a desolate rundown corner street pub. They stopped outside it.

Jez looked up and sighed. "Ah, this it, mate. The Odd Fellows Arms. I had me first pint in London here all those years ago. I haven't been back for years, man."

"All those years ago?" asked Miles "But you've only been down here three. Haha!"

Jez nodded. "Ah, I can see the confidence return to ya, young man. You're sounding cocky already and you've only just arrived here. Good to see it."

They walked in. There was a slight, but not overpowering, stench of stale cigarettes and beer. The once-resplendent white walls and high ceiling had now turned to an off-white nicotine yellow. This once-proud Georgian coach house was well into the twilight of its glory days and, as it appeared, so were the patrons. It seemed to Miles like the perfect marriage of convenience. The young barman stubbed out his cigarette and gestured towards Jez.

Jez moved closer to the bar. "Eh, yeah, two Stella's and a pack of cheese and onion, mate."

"And your little friend *is* over eighteen?" replied the barman with a slight smirk.

An uneasy look of guilt appeared on Miles' face. *This is Craig all over again. It's the beginning of the train journey and that old twat staring at me. For fucks sake, man, when will this stop?*

The barman turned towards Miles and laughed. "I'm just winding you up, mate. To be honest, I don't really care who I serve as long as they behave themselves. I'm paid fuck all anyway, so it's not as if I can really be arsed going around checking IDs now, is it?"

"No problems," said Miles, "but 'little friend'?"

A clearly irritated Jez picked up the drinks and walked towards a table by the door, then placed the drinks down harshly. Miles pulled his chair out and sat opposite him.

"Jez, man, I'm sorry if I looked a bit uneasy back there. But I've had a tough time today. I've been on edge all day 'cos of what I've done and can't relax. I'm convinced I'll get rumbled. Rumbled for anything from killing Craig, although I now know that I didn't, to who knows what? Oh yeah, he's not dead, by the way. I didn't tell ya that, did I?" The frantic pace of his output was beginning to increase.

"No man, ya didn't tell me that. That's great, man."

"Yeah, it is, right enough. It turned out that I just stunned him. Anyway, I've been edgy all day. Have I killed him? Have I not? What's Mum going to do? Has she called the cops? Has she not? If she has, are they on the train? Is that old man on the train one of them? Why is he looking at me and so on and so on?"

Jez leant forward, attempting to interrupt. "Miles!"

"Oh yeah, and you'll love this. I had to relax. I had to drink something. I just had to. And I know I'm just a little twat, a naïve little twat. I know that, but I managed to get served booze on the train. No bother. It was great. I just did it. Just went up there and said four cans of Stella. That's what I said. I just said it."

"Miles!"

"So there it is; that's why I'm on edge. That's why I seem all over the place. That's why I'm scared. That's why…" He looked up at Jez. "That's why. That's why. That I wish I hadn't done it; that I hadn't hit him. Well, I'm glad I hit him, but not like that. Yeah, anyway."

"Shut the fuck up, Miles," said a clearly irritated Jez. "Get a grip, man. You're okay. Chill, man. You'll be fine. You've got somewhere to stay. And you have money. You'll be fine. Nothing's gonna happen. Trust me. Me and Beanmonkey'll look after ya."

Miles looked up at Jez, puzzled. "Beanmonkey?"

"Yeah, Beanmonkey. Okay? He's my flatmate."

"Okay, but Beanmonkey?" asked Miles, trying to keep his laughter under check "Bean fucking Monkey? Haha!"

Jez, seeing the funny side, laughed back "Yes, Beanmonkey. You mad little fucker. Now shut up and drink. You pint's getting cold!"

* * *

Beanmonkey was driving at a frantic pace. He checked the time. It was five past four. *Fuck it! Fuck it. I'm late already. This is madness. It's crazy. What the fuck am I doing in* someone else's *shinny new Lexus? Then again, I wouldn't earn anything like this in a shitty little office job. And I certainly wouldn't get this rush!*

He then turned at speed, almost knocking into the back of a Tesco delivery van, down towards Wembley. *I hope this is it for at least a week. We're due a break. Two top of the range E-type jags and now this. All in a fucking week. Well, I'm sure he'll come up with something else, though, knowing him. Twat.*

Baskin, a career criminal, pimp and altogether, journey crime boss was standing opposite a lockup in a Wembley industrial estate.

Where is this little scroat? He mused. He looked at his tacky, chunky, gold-plated watch. *He's ten minutes late. He's a good lad, but he is ten fucking minutes late. Where is he?* Baskin, who, at the best of times, was highly impatient and a stickler for time keeping, wasn't a man who liked to be kept waiting. He looked at his watch again and kicked the garage door.

Beanmonkey sped into the industrial estate. In the near distance, he could make out the large silhouetted frame of Baskin standing by the lockup. *Oh, there he is, the lowlife. Baskin; that pathetic excuse for a human being. The epitome of all that's wrong with humanity. And he's so far in the closet I'm surprised he can still see. That dirty fucked up excuse for a man is my boss. Not exactly what I intended when I was deciding upon a career path. Now, Anton, let's see; what would you like to be one day? I know exactly what I want to be, someone who relieves hard-working people of valued possessions on the orders of a big, fat, closeted scum-bucket queen. Oh, if only me nan was alive; she'd be ever so proud.*

He pulled up opposite Baskin and stepped out of the car.

"Oh, hello, Jimmy," said a nervous-sounding Beanmonkey.

"How many times do I have to tell you?" Baskin scowled. "It's Mr. Baskin. Address me properly or suffer the consequences. Do I make myself clear?"

Inside, Beanmonkey was bubbling with rage. It seemed every time he met Baskin, he got that little bit closer to calling a halt to their association or, even worse, venting his anger. However, he knew that wasn't an option. He still had ambitions that he wished to fulfil, the fulfilment of which depended upon him avoiding falling prey to premature death. "Oh, I'm ever so sorry, Mr. Baskin. I truly am. That was so rude of me. I do apologise. It won't happen again."

This sickly, grovelling apology was carried out with the finesse of a seasoned actor, and he was, of course, acting. He had the type of charm and delivery about him that endeared him to those around him. Such was his panache and delivery of phrase that he could tell you to go to Hell and you'd look forward to the journey. He hated Baskin. However, such was his skilful discourse towards him that Baskin wasn't wholly aware of this fact. Beanmonkey didn't deal in transparency when it came to getting his feelings or point across to Baskin. This time, however, this contrite response was somewhat of a departure from his usual method of interaction with Baskin, and Baskin was slightly taken aback

After a slight pause, Baskin smiled. "Well, that's okay, Anton. We all make mistakes. I'll let this one go. We'll say no more about it. Now down to business." Baskin looked all around the car, then patted the roof. "You've done well, my son. Good work. That's top of the range. Who's my top boy? I tell you who is. You are. You never fail to deliver exactly what I ask for. Unlike that sheep shagger mate of yours, Jiz."

"It's Jez, actually, Mr. Baskin."

"That's right, Jiz. Anyway, last week I gave him instructions to get me a Boxster. I even gave him a map of the general location. I couldn't have made it any easier. What does he bring back? A Saab. A fucking Saab! Don't get me wrong, Saab's are quality motors, but it wasn't what I ordered. My clients are very particular. If they order something specific, that's what they expect to get. Anyway, luckily the dozy Arab agreed to take it off my hands."

Baskin opened the gates of the lock up. Beanmonkey got back in the car and drove it in. Franky, one of Baskin's hired hands, was on hand to greet him and the latest acquisition. Frankie was one of the nastiest, toughest and most ruthless men in the whole of West London. He was devoid of all conscience and attacked people with a sense of impunity, which suggested that he was beyond the reaches of the law. Beanmonkey got out of the car and went over to greet Frankie. *Keep smiling and pretend you're not absolutely shitting yourself, Beanie. He's like a dog; he can sense fear. He can fucking smell it! One sign of that and he'll have you. Only a few more minutes to go and you can smash some off down the Swan.*

Frankie looked at Beanmonkey, smirked, then looked at the car. "You've done well, Beanmonkey," he said mockingly. "Oh yeah, I've been meaning to ask, why do they call you that? I've never quite got that. Is it because 'monkey' rhymes with junkie? Ha ha."

If Baskin represented the thoughts, deeds and behavioural habits of everything Beanmonkey despised, then Frankie was the physical embodiment of it. He hated and despised people like him. These were the sort of people who preyed on the weak, vulnerable and trusting. His crowning glory and proudest hour had come when he broke both legs of Billy Danker, someone who owed Baskin money and who just happened to be a homosexual. He was the type of person who didn't have a conscience and seldom, if ever, showed remorse. Beanmonkey, through his association with Baskin, had known Frankie for three years and had hated him throughout. He never made it abundantly obvious to all around, only Frankie. It wasn't done in a smirking, smug unambiguous manner, but with a sublime subtlety. Beanmonkey had nothing but contempt for Frankie and Frankie knew it.

"Well," continued Frankie, "I hate to say this, but yeah, you've done all right. You've done all right, Junkie Monkey! Actually, Mr. Baskin, can I call him that instead of Beanmonkey from now on? Junkie Monkey, now that's got a much better ring to it. What do you think?"

"Leave the boy alone, Frankie," said Baskin, sounding uncharacteristically sympathetic. "He's done well today. In fact, he's done well all week. Anyway, down to business." He put his hand inside the left pocket of his tan-coloured crombie and produced a white envelope. "As I said, Anton, you've done well. There's a little something extra in there as a sign of appreciation. I'll be in touch."

Beanmonkey leant forward and took the envelope in his hand. "Thanks, Mr. Baskin. That's very kind of you. I'll wait to hear from you, then."

As he walked towards the gates, he stopped and turned to Frankie. "You take care now, Frankie. Actually, Frankie, I've been meaning to ask. Are you called Frankie because it rhymes with…? Actually, don't answer that. I think I know the answer!"

Although no longer religious, Beanmonkey had been brought up as a strict Catholic. He had done his stint as an altar boy, made his communion and been confirmed. Like all good Catholic boys, he'd had the dark demon of guilt stalk him all throughout his childhood. He'd been dragged off to church every Sunday and forced to go to confession periodically. All in all, he'd had a strong, solid grounding in all its rituals and tenets. Catholicism, like all major religions, tends to take a very dim view of suicide. Beanmonkey knew that, by his words to Frankie, he had gone very close to violating this sacred of tenets, but he didn't care. It seemed worth it.

* * *

In a semi-deserted Metropolitan line carriage on route to Wembley, Jez was waxing lyrical to Miles about his line of work, his aspirations for the future, his views on world peace and his friend, Beanmonkey.

Miles, being the logical, organised and pedantic person he was, liked to compartmentalise things. Sometimes he made a conscious decision to organise things in this manner; other times it was subconscious. In his compartmentalised mind, things had to make sense. Why shouldn't they make sense? What was the point if things didn't make sense? Not very logical, is it? What Miles didn't realise was that this uber-analytical obsession didn't always endear him to those around him. The split between those who thought he was simply a nerd and those who thought him interesting, though a bit unpredictable, was an equal split. To simply understand him as and label him as a nerd would be to miss the point. He was a clever, factual, off the wall, fragile soul. Or, to put it another way, a smart ass, know it all with a sensitive side. He was, at this moment, having great difficulty processing and compartmentalising the name Beanmonkey. Daft names were fine with him. He had no problems with daft names. Daft names, after all, were a term of endearment and served to set people apart from the otherwise-accepted norms. Simple though it was, Miles' favourite form of daft names was nicknames. The kind of nicknames that either derived from someone's surname, Banksey, Popkins or Smitthy, etcetera, or from their first names, Jez or Milesy, etcetera. Beanmonkey didn't, of course, fit either of these models, and this was causing Miles great distress. There was no tangibility between a bean and a monkey. Monkeys eat bananas, not beans. Whilst 'Bananamonkey' would make sense, that, also, was, nonetheless, silly. With logical understandings under attack, he could not take it anymore. It was all too much. He had to ask.

He looked up at Jez with a vacant, confused expression. A look that said 'please, can I ask you a question? Please, kind sir. I really must'.

Jez sighed. "Oh, what now, Miles? What's on that fragile little mind of yours?"

Miles composed himself. "Mate, I've got to ask. I know it's rude to stop someone in mid flow, but it's really bugging me. For what it's worth, I was enjoying your take on world peace and possible ways to bring it about, so I'm not doing this lightly."

Beanmonkey, who had been leaning forward amidst the throws of pronouncements, sat back and folded his arms in an indignant manner. "Haway, Miles, man. You poor, confused little man. What is this big question, then?"

Miles took a deep breath. "Beanmonkey. That's what I have a problem with."

"How can you have a problem with him if you haven't met him? Beannie's canny, man."

"Of course I don't mean the man. I mean the name," said Miles. "Why is he called Beanmonkey?"

"Are you for real, Miles?" asked Jez, sounding very astonished. "You really are a troubled little man, aren't you? Right then, Beanmonkey is slang for a very basic form of accountancy, right? In other words, even monkeys could do that. Anton, that's his real name, was kicked out of accountancy college for fuckin' up his exams. The other lads in class thought it would be funny to name him Beanmonkey."

"Ah," said Miles. "They were being ironic. I can see it now. Very clever. Anyway, yeah, sorry for being so rude again. Thanks for that." Miles, who had now had his troubling query answered, continued, "Anyway, so, the two of you rob cars, which have been pre-ordered. You're handed a list and on this list is a number of cars, which include their makes and models. You're then told to go out and find these cars and take them back to a psychotic nut job called Bustin?"

Jez nodded. "Baskin."

"Okay, Baskin. Anyway, this Baskin character then gives the car the once over and hands you an envelope full of notes."

Jez nodded and smiled in a way that denoted a strong sense of pride. "Yes, mate. That's about it. Yeah. But, last week, right, I had one motor left to get; it was a Boxter. You know, a Porsche Boxter. Baskin even gave me an idea of where to find it. Anyway, I eventually tracked it down. And what a top motor it was. Metallic grey; leather seats. You could almost smell the leather. Anyway, I go up to it. It's late, as well. There's no one around. I go up to it and, before I could even touch it, the alarm goes off. And I have to admit, for the first time since being involved in this kind of work..."

Miles laughed. "Work!"

"Yes, work," said Jez. "I nearly shat myself! Anyway, I am shitting myself and am frozen to the spot. The geezer looks out his window and shouts, 'oi, stay there'. Well, I didn't really have any choice in the matter, 'cos I couldn't move. The size of him, too; fucking huge. Anyway, I managed to get me head together and do one. All those boring fucking race meetings that my dad forced me to go on paid off in the end!"

"So what did you tell Baskin?"

"Well, I've been doing this long enough to know that if, you fail on your first attempt, don't keep trying the same motor. 'Cos people will be looking out for you. So you never go back. Move on to the next car. So I did the next best thing."

"Which was?"

"Get him something else. Okay, it mightn't be on the list, but it's a lovely motor all the same. I was on my way back to the flat and, just off Repton Avenue, I saw it."

"Repton Avenue?" asked Miles. "It's just a name to me."

"Yeah, it's not far from the flat. There it was in all its beautiful hand crafted and machine enhanced chrome, beauty it was. There it was, asking me, begging me to take it away from its mediocre middle-class suburban existence off to a new life of travel. A new and, albeit, possibly an unpredictable life."

Miles smiled. "That's beautiful, Jez. Really descriptive-like."

"Thanks. And there in all its glory it was. A Saab Turbo."

"You know what, Jez? That's lovely piece of descriptive commentary, but all that is waxing lyrical. All that descriptive prose for what? A Saab fucking Turbo?"

Jez replied, "You haven't got a clue about cars, have you? You're too young, I suppose."

"I'm only two and a half years younger than you."

"Indeed, my little friend! Haha! But two and a half years at our tender point in life is a long time. And let's face it. I am right. You know fuck all about cars. Generally speaking, like."

"True, I guess. But Saabs? I always thought they're big and clumpy."

"Not turbos, mate. Anyway, I nicked it the next night and brought it around to his lock up. And guess what? He loved it. He said that I showed a great ability to think on my feet and showed that I was very resourceful. He gave me an extra two hundred quid and invited me to go up London with him and a few of his mates. He said he can get us in anywhere in London. Any club, even the exclusive ones. Anyway, I couldn't go; I had arranged to meet Carla down the Swan."

"Who's Carla? Is she your bird? And the Swan?"

"Yeah, Carla's me bird. She's well fit. Actually, it was Baskin who introduced us. To be honest, even though he knows all these people and can get us into all these places, I try to keep my personal life separate. As I said, he's a nutter. He's even done time for murder." Jez looked up. "Ah, here we go. This is where we jump off."

Miles looked out the window at this dark, dreary station. Anxiety was now beginning to return to the mix.

"C'mon, Miles," said Jez, sounding impatient.

Miles jumped off the train. He was walking a few steps behind Jez. They both walked up the concrete stairwell. This new place, to Miles, had a slight feeling of hostility. As they walked towards the barriers, he noticed a stale stench of urine. Suddenly, a stark realisation that there was no turning back came over him. He had now come too far to turn back

Jez put his arm on Miles' shoulder. "So then, Miles. This is it. This is Wembley. Welcome to my world, Miles. Welcome to your new world."

Those words, 'welcome to you new world', had a strong resonance for Miles. The reality that he had embarked upon a new journey, a new voyage into the unknown had been punctuated by those words.

He looked around at Wembley High Street. It was too dark to give any definitive picture of what the place looked like. There was, however, a lurking sense of foreboding. Although he did realise that any new and busy place would serve to instil those very same feelings.

They walked past a kebab shop.

Jez turned to Miles. "You okay, mate?"

"Why? asked Miles. "Don't I seem fine? I haven't said anything. Actually, I'm not. I don't know why. As I said earlier, I haven't killed him. I just feel..."

"You just feel. Well, I think I can guess. You've stepped off the train in London. You've met me, then I've told you how I make my living, and now we're here. So yeah, I can guess how you're feeling, mate. Anyway, you'll be fine. London's a big, frightening place, but you've got a roof over your head and, as you say, you're sorted for cash for at least a few months. Then you can go back home when you feel more relaxed about stuff."

"But Jez," said Miles angrily, "I'm not going back. I can't now."

"That's up to you. But I think you will at some point. Anyway, for tonight, just try to relax. We'll have a few beers."

The flat inhabited by Beanmonkey and Jez was a modest two-bedroom, first-floor flat in a row of Victorian houses. There were two sofas with yellow throws over them, and a small coffee table. Play Station games and DVDs lay strewn across the floor. Sitting by the television was a shattered Beanmonkey. He was curled up in a comfy little ball, in the depths of thought. He knew that his line of work was fraught with danger and low on morality and, although remuneration was good, it was ultimately a life of subservience to a boss so unhinged that, at any moment, he could turn very nasty. It was only last year, after delivering a car an hour late, that Max Brystow over Pinner Way had received a very severe beating. The injuries from this beating with lead pipes, which had been ordered by Baskin and carried out by Frankie and two anonymous shaven-headed thugs, had taken a few months to recover from; fortunately, there had been no sense of urgency to be constantly earning, as Baskin paid very well. Despite this generous remuneration, Beanmonkey had briefly pitched the suggestion of possibly going it alone as they knew, by cutting out the middle man, they would make far more money; the idea was beached with the twin realisations that they didn't have Baskin's contacts and that Baskin would kill them. Literally.

* * *

Beanmonkey lighted another cigarette and sat back into the sofa. *What can Jez and I actually do? We set ourselves up as fairly decent people, but we're not. The people whose cars we steal are the decent people. They actually work hard for what they get. And what do we do? We take what they've worked hard for. Baskin talks shit. They're not all clueless snobs who've never had to struggle. Okay, some are. But, even if they are, so what? All that stupid inverted snobby that Baskin uses as a justification for this is complete bullshit. Baskin, yeah, we know that he's complete scum. But we work for him. We're nothing more than his foot soldiers. What does that make us? I work for a fucking psycho like Baskin. I fucking hate that twat. Well, I guess I've made my bed.*

"Ha ha. I am a fully paid up piece of scum! It's what I do. Fuck it!"

* * *

Miles was standing outside the kebab house while Jez ordered some much-needed, highly edible pieces of 'scraped off the floor cuttings of meat in a pita'. He was struck by the smell of stale food coming from the various food outlets. Bins were overflowing with rubbish and, from outside a nearby pub, a triangular-shaped piece stale vomit was stuck to the side of the wall.

Nice! Very nice, indeed! I'm out of my depth here, I really am. Why don't I just go back? I don't have to go back home. I could always stay with Aunt Grace; she hates Craig, too, and we seem to get on okay. I'm Miles Goodwin, a sixteen-year-old nerd. I'm only playing at being hard. It's not really me. All this 'hard man' stuff is just an act. It's not even as if I'll be in trouble. I haven't killed him. I haven't killed him. I'm glad I haven't killed him. I'm relaxed about that, but I have no idea what's ahead of me. How is a little nerdy, speccy self-opinionated twat from Carlisle meant to survive in London?

Jez came out of the kebab house carrying his purchase under his arm. "Right then, mate. Let's go."

They both turned and continued to walk down Wembley High Street.

Miles stopped abruptly. "Jez, can I be honest with you? And don't be pissed off, right?"

"Erm, yeah, I suppose. If you really must, like," replied a clearly irritated Jez.

"Okay, then," said Miles, gathering his thoughts. "Erm."

The longer it was taking Miles to get to the point, the angrier Jez was becoming "Just tell me, will you? Whatever it is, just tell me. You don't have to be nervous. C'mon, man."

"Okay, then. I don't think you should be doing what you do. I don't think you should be robbing cars for a living."

"You what? You've just arrived here. Nowhere to kip. I'm helping you out with a place to kip and you're having a go at what I do? You know you *do* have a choice. You could always piss off home. I didn't ask you to come. You called me. Remember?"

Miles shrugged. "Actually, I was thinking of heading back as it goes. I'm beginning to have second thoughts. I wasn't sure if I'd actually killed someone, but now I know I haven't. So yeah, you're right. I'll leave in the morning, if that's okay. And yeah, you have been very good to me. Cheers. Sorry."

"Look, man," said Jez, sounding guilty for his earlier retort, "you can stay as long as you want. I just thought it was a bit bang out criticising what I do, considering I'm helping you out."

"Yeah," replied an equally remorseful Miles. "It is. Sorry, it was a bit twatish. But I didn't mean it against you. I meant it against people like Bustin."

"For fuck sake, man. Baskin. It's Baskin. I don't like him, either, but at least get his name right."

"Yeah, sorry, Baskin. People like him are dangerous. They control the world you're in and can do what they want. They make the rules. They're nasty. I'm worried for you. Really worried. That's why I said it. No other reason."

"No that's fine, man. I understand. But don't worry. You don't need to. You know, anyway, I've been doing this for a couple of years. Long enough to know what I'm doing."

"But ya haven't. Knocking off warehouses in Carlisle and, yes, you were ace at that. But this isn't the same as working for a crime boss scum bag who could have you killed if he decides to in London; isn't the same."

"We've all got to earn a living and I earn a very good living doing what I do. I deliver what I'm asked to, take my money and leave, until the next time. He wouldn't touch me."

"So that's what he wants. He wants to know everything about your life. I mean, he's even decided what bird he wants you to see."

"Look, don't bring Carla into this, you know-it-all twat. Baskin introduced us, but the rest was up to us. Get it?"

"Yeah, obviously. But he still had some input."

"Well, he did have some input," said Jez, mimicking Miles. "Listen to yourself, man. You need to lose that toffee-nose shite if you're to survive here. It's a shit world. It's full of people like Baskin. It's full of people like me who've never known anything else. You need to toughen up if you're going to survive down here. Because if you keep saying what you want and expressing yourself..." He mimicked Miles. "...You'll drown. Seriously. So what's it to be? 'Cos if you decide that you don't want to lose this attitude, you may as well turn around and walk back to the station."

"I don't know what I want to do," said Miles. "Actually, it might be better just to go back. I think you're right; London's too big for me in every way. And, if I do go back, at least then I'll have the chance to finish my studies and get a proper job. Thanks for everything, mate." He smiled at Jez and stretched out his hand to grab Jez's hand. "I'm sorry for being such a knob." He turned around and starting walking towards the station.

"Look, Miles, don't be daft, man. If you go back now, he's won. Is that what you want? That fat twat with a smug grin on face. He'll never let you forget that he's won and that he's in charge. Haway Miles, man, come back."

* * *

In Sudbury town, a rather nondescript township of Wembley, Beanmonkey stood opposite one his favourite places in his world. This place, to him, was a parallel universe. It was a place where dreams could be constructed, and theories put forward from why the offside rule was no longer relevant to the beautiful game, to why we're not convinced that Princess Diana wasn't killed by MI5. It was a place where worries about one's relevance to society and one's place therein could be laid to waste under a sea of compulsive over consumption. Once you stepped over that gripper plate, you were there. Feelings of guilt, smugness and a desire to embrace honesty had no currency.

The Swan, with its wonderfully imposing Gothic-style façade, which included pillars either side of the main entrance, had an inviting yet underlying dark feel to it.

He walked through, surveying all in sight. Over to the left, by the pool table and bending over provocatively, was Sasha Burstill. Sasha, because of her penchant for tight-fitting jeans and low-cut tops, was considered easy and cheap by certain patrons. Ironically, the patrons who considered her as such were the ones who never got to experience that side of her. Not because they held such views; she was oblivious to them. It was quite simply because she wasn't attracted to them. She was, however, very much attracted to Beanmonkey, but he wasn't interested. He'd already had her. Twice. More than twice, then you're in potentially difficult territory, was his rationale. It was all down to frequency and the number of times one slept with someone. If this simply flirtatious equation was tampered with or the boundaries pushed, then the lines of carefree and noncommittal, and the beginnings of a relationship became blurred. Beanmonkey didn't do relationships. He did fun.

Sitting in the centre of the bar area was Big Greg Towser. He was the type of person who was everyone's friend. Or so he thought. Actually, he was delusional. People liked him all right, but only when he put his hand in his pocket to rack up a round of drinks. He mistook, or rather, chose to mistake, their subsequent gratitude for universal friendship. He felt part of their club. He felt part of something bigger than himself. The reality was, he'd arrive alone, take his usual stool, then pull it up to the bar. He'd then deliver the 'usual, please' line to whoever was serving. A glass, his glass, emboldened with some kitsch image of a drunk alongside his name, was filled with his choice of drink. 'Old Sherlock' was, in fact, the only drink he ever ordered. If he didn't recognise anyone to whom he could bestow a drink upon, he stayed by himself for the entirety of his visit. He always left alone.

These two, apart from Kevan, the barman, were the only recognisable faces. The students from the nearby college of technology were in, but he didn't recognise any of them. Apart from a small select group, they were largely a transient lot who spread their disposable income very thinly on the ground.

Beanmonkey walked over to the bar. "Hi, Kev. Can I get the usual, please?"

Greg looked around.

"Sorry, Greg, mate. Cheap shot! Actually, today I'll have the Monkey, please."

"What?" asked Kevan. "A bit early, isn't it? It's not even six yet. You usually reserve these for the weekend, and even then it's only towards the end of the night."

"Well," said Beanmonkey, "I've got a few days off and I've been given a nice little bonus, too."

"Aha, so how is life in the travel business, then? Obviously paying well," said Kevan.

Kevan turned and walked over to the back of the bar to begin to blend the ingredients necessary for the creation of the 'Monkey'.

To have the respect of the majority of the patrons in the subterranean confines of the public house was an honour. Securing that honour and the time in which that honour was forthcoming was generally down to the individual. Some people, due to their charismatic refrain and general conviviality, seemed to secure it after relatively few visits. Others, through simply belligerent perseverance and dogged attention to the accumulation of appearances, achieve this over time. This honour is potentially open to everyone in the confines of this world. All start with a level playing field. If certain simple rules of engagement and situational ethics are observed, the honour is eventually bestowed. To not receive this honour, one has to express, whether through one's behaviour or through a decided indifference, that's it not desired. In short, it's easier to acquire this honour than it is to not acquire it. To have a cocktail named after oneself, however, is a privilege.

Miles and Jez were just coming onto Sudbury High Street.

"So, Miles," said a much calmer and relaxed Jez, "what do you think? Welcome to Sudbury."

Although decidedly more relaxed and resigned to his new fate, Miles wasn't sure what to think. He had long dispensed with the paranoia of a possible manslaughter and subsequent prison sentence hanging over him. He had taken his first steps in London and, in so doing so, had confined his metropolitan virginity very willingly to history. He had survived what had to have been one of the unhealthiest kebabs he had ever tried. Not unhealthy in the sense that kebabs are harvested from the cuts of meat that dare not speak its name, but in a sense of the putrid surroundings in which it had been produced. Miles had never seen so many dead flies stuck to a butcher's heater. And what did he think of Sudbury? He wasn't sure. Well, he certainly wasn't impressed with what he was witnessing. His problem was expressing this in a way that wouldn't make him come across like an ungrateful, judgmental belligerent little snob. This was going to be difficult. Miles was both articulate and resourceful, but he was struggling. He could, of course, lie.

"Yeah, man," said Miles, trying his best to come across enthusiastic. "Urban. It's got a real stark, urban vibe to it. Yeah, it's cool, man. I love the way there's litter everywhere. Cans and newspapers blowing around. It's all there. Yeah, man. I'm feeling it."

Being able to take a lie and pass it off as a truth, to pass it off as original opinion, is not an easy thing to achieve. This was an extremely poor attempt on behalf of Miles.

"Urban vibe." Jez laughed. "Haha. That's good, man. I like it."

They walked up to the Swan.

"Miles, mate, just stop for a second and take a good look. Have you ever seen such pillars before? It's quite canny. Don't you think?"

Miles didn't have to even attempt to construct a lie this time. He was a big fan of architecture of all periods and styles, in particular Georgian and Gothic. A contradiction, of course, but Miles summed it up perfectly.

"Indeed, mate. I'm well impressed. I love the stark beauty of it all."

They walked in and saw Beanmonkey over by the bar talking to Kevan.

"Eh, Jez, man," said Beanmonkey. "So this is Miles? The little tearaway. Well, mate. Welcome to Sudbury. What can I get you both?"

"Well," said Jez, "seeing as you're drinking one, how about getting us a couple of Monkeys?"

"Monkeys?" asked Miles.

"It's a cocktail consisting of vodka, Kahlua, Tia Maria and tequila topped off with a dash of coke," said

Beanmonkey.

"Yes, but why is it called Monkey? That's a bit weird."

"Because, my little friend," said Beanmonkey proudly, "it was named after me. Anyway, get a table and I'll bring them over."

Miles and Jez walked past the pool table. As they were walking past, Sasha Burstill flashed Miles a cheeky smile. He smiled back. Things appeared to be improving the longer the day progressed. He was now finding it hard to regret ever hitting Craig. On the contrary, he was beginning to wonder why he hadn't done it before. Not necessarily hit Craig over the head with a wok. That was just instinct and survival coming to the fore, and an act unlikely to be repeated. No, he was wondering why he hadn't made the move South before now. After a year in London, Jez had offered to put him up should the need or sense of adventure ever arise. He was here now. That was what mattered. The last remnants of foreboding were leaving him. He looked around at his new surroundings. His role of fugitive on the run from justice, to a teenager in the throws of discovery, was now becoming very apparent. His happy exterior displayed this as he took his seat.

Jez, noticing this, smiled, too, and gave him a reassuring pat on the back.

"Things will be fine, mate. We'll look after you and see you right. Even though all the lads back home think that Jez lad's reet hard and all that, I was scared when I came down here. Only, if you tell anyone, I'll have to give you a kicking! Only joking. But yeah, it's scary at first, but you'll just eventually blend in and be part of things. I'm proud of you, man."

This was both a special and powerful moment for Miles. Here was a person who he had idolised as the perfect role model, the person all teenagers should aspire to become, or at least try to become. He was the epitome of a teenage dream role model. Now here he was laying bare his protective side. There was no forced 'hard man' bravado here, just plain, honest emotion. Miles was incredibly moved and taken aback by this display. He so desperately wanted to cry. This wasn't an option.

Beanmonkey walked over with the drinks

"So, Miles, the wok man! Haha! That cracked me up! Nice one, mate."

Miles smiled. "Ah, well. Yeah, I can laugh now, but I wasn't at the time. I thought I'd killed him. It turns out that I only stunned him. He's okay now, according to me mum. Yeah, it is funny. One minute, I'm on the train absolutely shitting myself; the next, this man here is amusing me with the various car crime-related stories. Haha!"

Beanmonkey turned towards Jez. "You told him, then? Nice one."

"Ah, c'mon, Beans," said Jez. "It's Miles. I know him. He's canny."

Suddenly, the need for Miles to return the favour and protect Jez became apparent.

"No, man, it's fine," said Miles. "I'm not a grass. I think, on one hand, it's funny, but, on the other, it's tragic. It's as if I've walked onto the set of a London gangster flick. People do what they have to survive, I guess. It's not just down to 'is this right or wrong'? That's a whole new subject. No, it's down to asking yourself, the inner you, 'what can I make the most money at'? What am I good at? After a while, then you may decide whether you'll continue with it or perhaps try something new and something that doesn't have all the hassles and questions of what you're doing now."

"Miles. You haven't lost your ability to talk shite, then," said Jez.

"I don't know, Jez, mate," said Beanmonkey. "I'm hearing very wise words coming from the mouth of someone far too young to say 'em. There's a lot of food for thought there."

"Food for thought!" said Jez. "Umm, perhaps some, I guess. Perhaps some."

3

Anton Jeremiah Smithson

The emotion of guilt is one of the most powerful and destructive emotions there are. If one allows it to be the master, it can drain the person holding that emotion of all rationale and clarity of action. If, on the other hand, one retains control, one has the ability to harness its powers and use it to achieve results that would otherwise have been unachievable. However, an emotion with no patently positive properties is regret. Regret serves only to remind one of one's mistakes and shortcomings of the past. To make the party go with a bang and to add that extra spice, the emotion of anger is invited to come along. Beanmonkey was at the beck and call of all three emotions. Most of the time, they didn't bother him. However, they were merely lying dormant in wait for the perfect opportunity to pounce. Each time he stole a car, a net salary of guilt was saved to his memory bank. He did have ways of dealing with this guilt, which everyone knew about. There were the drugs. Marijuana, usually, or the odd ecstasy tablet, were employed for this purpose, and, very occasionally, a line or two of cocaine. As well as drugs, there was music and sex. Being handsome and a reasonable guitarist meant that sex was easily obtained, though he usually came away from playing the guitar less than completely satisfied. All this, however, served only to postpone the guilt. It was still there waiting for him, though in a somewhat less acute form. He also had another way, a secret way, of dealing with his guilt. If one method was based on diving head first into hedonism, this was done by embracing penance. He didn't feel anyone needed to know. Actually, he didn't want anyone to know; except, of course, the beneficiaries of this guilt. To them, he was just a do-gooder volunteer doing his bit for society. Humility would not sit easily alongside his nonchalant persona. So, when he had a spare day, he'd jump on the Tube to Rayners Lane and lend a hand at St. Jerome's home for the elderly. His thinking here was that, by downloading a bit of penance in the shape of good deeds, this would counteract the previously downloaded guilt. After putting in a full day at Jerome's, he felt absolved. This would last until the next time he was behind the wheel of an illegally acquired motor vehicle.

There was something else bothering him. Something Miles had said. In fact, it was a few things he had said. *What did he mean that it's not just about right or wrong, then, on the other hand, say it's tragic,* he thought. *How can it be okay, but also tragic? The funny thing is that, in some strange way, what he said seemed to make perfect sense. Most people far older than me, never mind him, don't make half the sense he seemed to make last night.*

He pulled the front door shut and walked out the gate. It was bitterly cold. Along the way, he could make out the frozen blob of Miles' pavement gift from the night before. *It wasn't really fair to make him match us shot for shot,* he thought. *He's only a kid.* He turned towards the bleak, deserted urban landscape of Sudbury High Street. He was looking forward to consigning this by now irritating and niggling guilt to history. He wasn't sure if he hated himself more for his actions or for the guilt he felt as a result of these actions. It wasn't easy being a flawed highly virtuous person.

It's quite often the case that, the stricter one's up bringing, the more wayward that person will become. This was true in the case of Beanmonkey.

As soon as he found himself away from home studying, it was as if a giant weight had been lifted from his shoulders. The old rule book governing morality, a sense of duty, accountability – ironically– and all the other societal bylaws was revised and rewritten. He felt liberated from it all. The only tenet that was retained was the sense of fair play that had been instilled in him by his strict Methodist father. Although brought up in the religious practices of his mother's Catholicism, his father had instilled the upstanding socio-religious accountability of the Wesleyite persuasion. The sense of fair play of starting from a level playing field, as his compatriots, had been paramount in his everyday dealings. Whether that was in sport, at home or simply in friendship, it was observed. Perhaps, more accurately, the sense of fair play was the last remaining tenet that he aspired to and, by his own standards, fell that little bit short of. He no longer gave it unbending observance. In his mind, although he longed for a purity of observance to it, he realised that, in fact, it was beyond his reach. Aspiring to something that, these days, seemed to be beyond his reach wasn't the same as living by it. This was an ongoing dilemma.

He wished that he could be the kind of person he was about to become today, every day. Most people didn't have to placate their conscience by making moralistic gestures. Most people didn't give themselves cause to have to do so in the first place. The problem with Beanmonkey was that the financial lure of continuing along this path of unrighteousness was much too strong for him to resist. So, by continuing as a small cog, albeit a vital one in this illegal venture, and then carrying out the resulting self-imposed penance, a compromise was reached.

St. Jerome's home for the elderly was, to the outside observer, a depressing place to experience. Its patrons seemed resigned to a fate of mere existence, some even giving off a desire for the advent of death to be hastened. Looking at the surroundings in which they played out this existence, it wasn't difficult to see why. The employees, with a few exceptions, seemed indifferent to all this. It was as if they had desensitised themselves to their surroundings and were operating on auto-pilot. Although employed in the caring profession, it wasn't difficult to see why most of them didn't do it out of a sense of vocation. It wasn't like being a doctor or a nurse, where the currency was the chance to prolong life. The currency here was death, and the facilitation of as smooth a passage to it as possible. This in itself was potentially soul destroying, which went some way towards explaining their apathy. To Beanmonkey, however, this whole resignation to the finality of it all wasn't necessary. Everyone knew what the end result would be; that was beyond question. He just couldn't understand the willingness to simply let nature take its course. This, to him, was more like a hospice than an old folks' home.

Why do I do these things, he wondered. *I wouldn't have to be going all the way to an old folks' home to offload all this if I led a normal life like anyone else. I just hope this passes soon. It's really beginning to piss me off.*

The length of time it took for normality to resume varied a lot. It could take anything from two days to a week. However, this horrible cocktail of guilt-panic-regret, which, in turn, resulted in a mild form of depression, always went. The length of time it took to leave depended upon its initial severity.

On a normal given day, Beanmonkey was the exact opposite of the skulking, depressed-looking lost soul he now was. He was confident and arrogant, and paraded around like a strutting peacock. This was Beanmonkey at his very finest, at his truest. Again, he wondered when normality would resume. The irony here was that he found it easier to be nice to those around him when he felt himself. To him, there was no contradiction between being arrogant whilst being caring and helpful. It was when he was at his lowest, drained of self-worth and overdosing on self-loathing that he became the kind of person people would do well to avoid. He didn't think that, in order to experience humility, one had first to be stripped of pride. Being overly arrogant in everything allowed him to be himself. When he was himself, he felt happier. When he felt happier, he was a better person.

In the drab surroundings of St. Jerome's, Jane Tollafield was bringing in Arthur Seagrove's dinner. Today was his favourite. He always enjoyed Wednesdays, as that was curry and rice day with treacle pudding to follow.

Arthur was an 'old trooper', as those who knew him liked to refer to him. It was a well-earned term of endearment. Not only did he have an unbending spirit of enthusiasm and, despite his surroundings, a joy of life, he was a proud veteran of the D-day landings. The one usual manifestation of pride he allowed himself was recounting various anecdotes of these times. However, nothing came close to the annual Remembrance Day commemorations. It would all start off at 7 a.m. Whoever was on duty at the time would help him into the bath. He'd then gaze with immense pride at his blazer, with all his perfectly polished medals adorning it. He'd skip breakfast and lunch, as, for him, this was his small way of remembering the discomfort he and his fallen comrades had felt back then. The eleventh minute of the eleventh hour of the eleventh month was both the proudest and saddest time of his year. He had many stories to tell, and Beanmonkey would listen to them all with great patience, over and again.

Jane knocked on the door. "Arthur, you awake?"

"Of course I'm bloody awake, woman," replied Arthur.

Jane brought in his tray and set it down on his bed. She sat at the side of his bed, looked at him and smiled. "You know, Arthur, people like you make it worthwhile and a pleasure to work here. So a big happy birthday to the old soldier. So, how are you feeling? How many is this now?"

"Don't patronise me, woman. Yes, I'm fine. I've just got a bit of a sore head. I don't know why. I was feeling fine earlier, then bang. It just hit me. Knocked me for six, it did. And you know exactly how old I am. Do we have to go through the same routine every year? Blimey, woman."

Arthur was, of course, being very tongue in cheek with Jane. Jane cared deeply for him and there was a very strong bond between them. He enjoyed this annual routine where she asked his age and he, in turn, feigned indignation. If it didn't happen, he'd feel genuine indignation.

"Don't get yourself over excited now, love," said Jane. "You know what the doctor said about your high blood pressure. You really have to start looking after yourself; you're no spring chicken."

"Ha. And you are? I mean, how old are you now – fifty-two?"

"That's a good comeback, my love. Just shows that there's still fight left in the old man. Oh, did I tell you that nice young man, Anton, is popping in to wish you happy birthday?"

"No," replied Arthur in mock surprise. "Has he been nicking motors again?"

"Has he been what?" answered a startled Jane.

"Don't mind me, I'm going mad, Jane. Just mumbling nonsense to myself. I mean, I am old, aren't I? No spring chicken. Chicken."

Jane shrugged. "That's so true, my love. So true." She bent, kissed him on his forehead and walked out.

This had been a close call. If Jane hadn't dismissed Arthur's mumbling as the mere ramblings of someone approaching senility, then a trust, a covenant between two mutual confidants, would have been severely compromised, even broken.

Beanmonkey was the one person who sat patiently through Arthur's various long, involved and heart-rending accounts. He did this for a number of reasons, mostly because he liked and admired Arthur. Also, being the patriotic person he was, he had the utmost respect for someone who was willing to sacrifice themselves for their country. He also genuinely found his accounts, especially the war-based ones, fascinating and captivating. He was strongly of the opinion that any film, book or play that he had come across, or had yet to come across, couldn't come close to what Arthur had to recount. These, after all, were true accounts from someone who had been there, from someone who had risked life and limb for his fellow men and women. These weren't just stories, but powerful lessons, lessons in humility and respect, and an overall insight into the human condition. Beanmonkey loved them. Also, coming in to speak to Arthur provided a welcome respite from cleaning up faeces and wiping vomit from the mouths of the less fortunate residents. Arthur was well aware of the esteem with which his young friend held him, and being able to recount the many chapters of his life to a willing listener without hindrance was a much-needed tonic. Arthur, in turn, played the good listener, and this was a valuable source of release for Beanmonkey. There was a genuine affection and bond between them. It was a bond that neither party wished to see compromised.

* * *

In London's Embankment, Miles and Jez were standing opposite a red double-decker tour bus.

Jez shook his head and turned to Miles. "Miles, man, are you really sure you want to do this? It's a bit clichéd, don't ya think?"

"A bit. Yeah, I agree. But it's no more clichéd than a small town hood who comes to London and hooks up with gangsters. I mean, a bit Oliver Twist, don't ya think?" asked Miles jokingly. "Without, of course, the small town hood bit."

Jez laughed and nodded in recognition. "Yeah. 'Spose so."

Deciding to go on a clichéd open-top, red, double-decker tour of London was a tongue and check gesture on the part of Miles, but it was also something from which he derived some sense of adventure. Although he had only seen Wembley and Sudbury briefly and at night, he still hadn't a strong feeling he was in London. These places could have been suburbs of any fairly sizable town. There was nothing particularly 'Londonesque' about them. Today, unapologetically, was all about him. It was all about Miles finding his bearings. It was all about Miles finding his own canvas and painting his own impressions upon it. He was now sitting on the top seat of the high Church of Uber London, with Jez observing patiently. In a way, this was a big risk for Miles. He wasn't long in London and, in that short time, he had gone from a frightened, unsure figure to an excited adventurer. Luckily for him, Jez didn't appear to mind being subject to his whims.

Miles was endowed with a great sense of imagination. He used to love re-enacting what he imagined were great battles on a Sunday when his dad took him out to the Roman wall when he was younger. He missed his dad. He wondered what he would make of all this. In particular, he wondered what he would make of him hitting Craig over the head and thinking he'd killed him. *He'd probably laugh*, he thought. *Dad had a great sense of humour.*

Straight ahead, he could see the house of parliament directly in front of him. To the side was the London eye. He smiled. This couldn't have been more textbook for him and exactly what he wanted. The bus started up and pulled out onto Embankment. He felt a slight spray of rain as he looked out onto the Thames. This light drizzle was enhancing the experience. He sighed and sat back. Jez placed his headphones in position as advised to do by the tour guide, and beckoned to Miles to do the likewise. Miles shook his head to signify that he wouldn't be following suit. He wanted to observe and draw his own conclusion.

Beanmonkey, after bringing in ten different dinners to patients, emptying four bed pans, cleaning vomit off a bedroom floor and playing peacemaker in an altercation over what should be watched on television, was now sitting in Arthur's room. The visit to Arthur signified the last leg of his penance and a welcome respite.

"I'm not sure if I get this anymore, Anton," said Arthur. "If it plays that much on your conscience, then why don't you stop?"

"But I can't," replied Beanmonkey, sounding agitated. "I know it's wrong. But it's all I know and I'm good at it. It's what I do."

"It's what I do. It's all I know. Listen to me, matey. It's not as if you're too old to go back to accountancy school and finish what you started. You can even use your ill-got gains to fund it. You've done well out of it, as you say."

"Yeah, I could, but it's not as simple as that."

"Of course it is. Think of today. You're here doing penance for something that you didn't have to do. Either harden up and desensitise yourself to it like the rest of the scum who don't give two hoots for their victims, or leave this game. It's a simple choice. I have a lot of time for you, Anton. You're the one person who will sit through my endless litany of stories. You give me that time. Yes, some of the others listen, but they're only pretending to be interested. That's why I can't understand how someone so bright and gifted with the conscience that you've been gifted with continues to do what you do. What was it is that young lad said to you yesterday?"

"It was really weird. He said that we all had to make a living. That we have to do what we're best at, but he said it was tragic all the same. Does that make sense to you, Art? Because, on one hand, yes, it makes sense that we should do what we're good at. I am good at nicking motors. Very good, in fact, but then why say it's tragic?"

"I don't know. Maybe he's asking if there's something else you can turn your hand to. Anyway, why do the words of a sixteen-year-old affect you so much?"

"I don't know why. They just do. Another thing is that, if I do leave, Baskin will come after me and, let's just put it this way. He'll extract his pound of flesh."

"Extract his pound of flesh? That's what I'm taking about. I mean, how many people in your game would be able to quote the bard?"

"Not many. I guess."

"As for his pound of flesh. I've got a way around that."

"You have?" replied a startled Beanmonkey.

* * *

This had been a strange rebirth for Miles. Although he imbibed everything this perceived newfound independence had to offer, he still felt as if he was far short in reaching the full gestation period. Here he was riding high on an open-top, red, double-decker bus, but who was he? Who did he actually think he was? Had he done the right thing?

He couldn't help thinking that his overall decision to leave his home and Carlisle was something he may still come to regret. There was no going back once the break had been made, and no amount of bustling streets and dodgy older friends would make the slightest bit of difference in all of this. He had to make a success of his life, and, if he didn't, it would all be down to him and him alone. Buy now; pay later. Reap what you sow. Act in haste and pay at leisure. What was it all for? Did he really think that hitting Craig, then running away, was something that had benefited his mother? Was his motivation behind hitting Craig one of protection for his mum, or had he actually done so for himself to provide a cast-iron reason for embarking upon a journey that he had wanted to take since the sad demise of his father? He had made his bed now and he had no choice but to lie in it.

He had to gather his thoughts. He knew himself well enough to know that, once a downward spiral of thought had begun, it was difficult to get back on track. Besides, it was very inconsiderate to his highly patient new mentor.

He tried to dwell on the positive. He had seen a lot of London in a just few hours. Moreover, he had seen a lot of what he perceived London to be in a few hours. All throughout, Jez had remained patient and accommodating to the wishes of his new guest.

The bus pulled up at a stop in Park Lane, and they both stepped off into the light autumn drizzle

In a gesture of baptism, Miles lifted his head to catch the oncoming droplets of rain. The arrival of each drop was greeted with a shake of the head. He looked across the road at the park and walked towards it. There was a soft, soothing wind blowing through the trees, which acted as a fitting soundtrack to what he was seeing. Despite it being not much later than 3:30 p.m., it was becoming decidedly overcast and the street lamps within the park were gradually being called into action.

Miles was enjoying his London experience. They both were. Despite having lived in London for years, Jez had never visited Hyde Park. In fact, he had only ever seen a fraction of what they had both seen today. Miles was kicking up the brown autumn leaves as he walked along. All feelings of paranoia and stress had left him. The fresh autumn air and the fumes coming from the busy rush-hour traffic of Park Lane formed a nice urban cocktail.

* * *

Beanmonkey stood opposite St. Jerome's and smiled. He had worked hard today, spoke candidly and listened intently to some heartfelt advice. He felt absolved and cleansed of all wrong doing. He smiled again. His swagger had returned as he sauntered back towards Rayner's Lane tube station. He felt proud of what he'd achieved today and, once again, he felt good about himself. This was all a far cry from his earlier feelings of self-loathing and lack of worth. He was again a valuable member of society until, of course, the next crisis of conscience beset him. Today, however, was different from all previous visits. Today, he had been handed an opportunity to potentially escape this destructive cycle of events. There was a lot to consider. Yes, his life was going to change if he was to pick up the gauntlet thrown down by Arthur. His life was in need of changing. He knew this. Despite his single mindedness in continuing to remain in his current line of business, he had a probing conscience, which refused to stay silent. Change, now more than ever, seemed necessary and essential.

4
Jimmy Baskin

Baskin didn't like having to answer awkward questions. He didn't like being put on the spot. If one told a lie, then other lies needed to be constructed in order to keep track of the original lie. This wasn't easy. Quite often, discrepancies in these stories will help unravel this original mistruth. If one leads a double life, or, in Baskin's case, a triple life, this subterfuge is fraught with great difficulty.

Baskin lived in Harrow on the Hill in a modest six-bedroom mock Tudor mansion. The driveway was covered in pebbles and a collection of other stones, which made a swishing and crunching sound whenever cars drove in. He loved that sound. He had done so ever since he was a teenager. He had heard this great sound effect resonate in his mind since then, and wanted not only to hear that sound every day, but, moreover, wanted everything that sound represented. To him, it represented wealth and success. The sound itself was very pleasing to the ear, but it was more about what it represented.

He pulled up slowly to the gates of his house, pressed the buzzer, waited the few seconds for the strong steel gates to recline, then drove in. He drove in at speed to maximise this swishing sound, then ground to a sudden halt. He did this whenever he was excited. He was excited today, but was also apprehensive. Being present at and personally helping to carry out the severe beating inflicted upon Danny Hall for a late delivery of an E-type Jaguar had made him late. Whenever he was late, Natasha, his beautiful trophy wife, would ask him a string of awkward questions in quick succession. This made him uneasy, even though he always had a watertight cover story. Baskin's life of truth was tenuous, at best, and, at worst, tenacious, depending, of course, on one's standpoint.

His third life, if uncovered by his doting twenty-eight-year-old former 'Miss Pinner', would have presented an even bigger dilemma than his second. This secret side was an added fondness for a 'love that dare not speak its name'. He liked sex with men. Young men. Handsome men. Tall men. Slim men. Men with chiselled features and the clichéd body of an Adonis. Men who, in his mind, didn't look gay. He couldn't have that. After all, he was homophobic. No. He liked strong men. Macho men. The type of men who would hold the door open for a lady. Manners were very important to Baskin.

He didn't think he was doing anything morally wrong. Nothing distasteful in that apart from the obvious lack of fidelity to one's spouse, one would think. However, as was Baskin's want, it wasn't that simple. Due to his sadistic and controlling nature, it had a sinister angle.

These objects of Baskin's desire were procured by his hired thugs. They were brought to his warehouse under menaces, which generally included threats of a physical nature to their person, or, more distastefully, implied threats to other members of their families if they didn't comply. The police weren't a problem, as, due to the stigma of and the reporting of male rape and the fear of imminent harm coming to their loved ones, reporting such brutality wasn't a fear Baskin had to contend with, never mind consider. He was above the law and morally impervious.

To those with whom he shared a professional association, he was a ruthless bully whose personality bordered on the psychotic. To his wife, he was a strong, moral family man with a successful import-export agency. This was, of course, partially true in that the export of commodities played an essential part of his business dealings. It was what he exported that was the issue here. Natasha was under the impression that it ranged from anything from clothes to art. She liked the fact that it was art, as this heralded to her the arrival and acceptance into a club she had always wanted to be part of. She was the consummate social climber. He was a considerate lover, attentive spouse, doting father to their three-year-old girl and the rock upon which her privileged lifestyle stood. He was a man of class. A successful man. He was a man who could hold his own in intellectual discourse with the best of them. He was an importer and exporter of art. He went shooting with the elite and he was a Freemason. He knew which wine went with what. They took four holidays a year, one in their peak district retreat and three abroad. She loved him. She trusted him. He appreciated opera. They went to the opera. He never had problems getting tickets to the opera. Be it Covent Garden or La Scala. That's right, they'd been there, too. He knew people, you see. He knew lots of people. He knew the right kind of people. The people who could do anything, the people who could get anything and the people who could do anyone.

This balding, fifty-six-year-old, overweight former council estate bin man had it all and Natasha knew it. They were having people around that evening for dinner, followed by Backgammon. Baskin liked Backgammon.

He got of out of his top-of-the-range, unnecessarily large Land Rover and slammed the door behind him. He knew the questions would come thick and fast, and he also knew that he wasn't in the correct frame of mind to provide perfect answers. He was tired. He was mentally drained. There had been no need for him to get involved in the brutal retribution, which had been handed out to Danny Hall. Greg and Frankie had had that in hand. However, he had felt compelled to get involved. He personally wanted to get involved. Getting involved was essential, really. It was a given. His personal involvement in this retribution was paramount, he felt. A strong message, with himself as the chief signatory, had had to be delivered. Due to his warped rationale, he felt as if he had been the victim, not the person who had undergone a serious beating.

He sighed and put his key in the door. As he turned his key, the door opened and Natasha greeted him with a loving embrace. He was slightly taken aback by this. This was a pleasant surprise for him. Not only did he not have to be on his guard, fending off and deflecting the stinging questions that, otherwise, would have come his way, he could get on with the welcome business of relaxing.

Hold on a sec, he thought, *How come she's all right? All lovey dovy. It's good, though. But I don't understand. Anyway, fuck it. It's all good!*

* * *

Beanmonkey was sitting behind the wheel of a Lexus IS 250 Auto. He had been looking forward to this one ever since snatching the list from Baskin's grubby hands. In fact, his eyes lighted up as soon as he saw it. Such was his overwhelming excitement at the prospect of such a beautiful challenge that he didn't even attempt to feign nonchalance. Baskin liked seeing the expression of joy and delight on his employees' faces, and he smiled at Beanmonkey's reaction. When they took the list home, it was generally down to Beanmonkey to divide it up between them. As Jez quite frankly didn't really care one way or another which car he stole, Beanmonkey got to drive his favourites. Although fraught with risk and subject to the whims of his conscience, this was, in a way, any boy's dream job and he gleaned whatever glamour and excitement he could from it. After all, it wasn't generally long after the event that guilt crashed violently into his fragile conscience. Therefore, it was important for him not just to enjoy the moment, but the overall build up, too. The words of advice from Arthur Seagrove were niggling irritatingly at the back of his mind, but he didn't care. He'd have plenty of time to address these later whilst dealing with the obligatory guilt, but no, for this moment, he didn't care too much. Here he was behind the wheel of the Lexus IS 250 Auto. Maximum speed 150 MPH, acceleration at 6.2 MPH, fuel injected and power steering. This was a joy to drive. A veritable motoring treat, Alloy wheels, chrome dashboard and sleek black body. Beanmonkey was smitten. He turned onto Clapham High Street. It was important to maintain a reasonable speed so as not to draw attention to himself. After all, the middle-aged legal owner wouldn't be back until five, which gave him four hours, and he'd been careful and made sure that he wasn't seen. Getting in had been child's play. It had been one of the easiest acquisitions yet. Painstaking surveillance had been carried out, and the movements of the victim and times thereof noted. This job was part car thief and part detective. The detection part of the job was just as important as the driving. As soon as he saw the victim leave for work at his local estate agent's office, he calmly walked over to the car and inserted the knife into the side of the window. This time, it was effortless. The slimjim slid in with blissful ease, Beanmonkey jumped in and, with a little adjusting of the ignition chamber wires, was off. It was perfect.

He wasn't one for banal mundane things, so it had been no surprise when he had lost his place on the accountancy degree course. His parents were, of course, disappointed at the time, but, in truth, weren't overly surprised. He had tried to feign a degree of interest necessary for the successful completion of the course, but his heart really wasn't in it. This was plain for all to see and, in all honesty, his parents knew. They had hoped that he would somehow muster even the most basic pretence of enthusiasm necessary for successful completion and subsequent entry into a nice, safe suburban existence, but this wasn't Beanmonkey. It wasn't who he was. It wasn't what made him tick and, despite a desire to please others, he just wasn't able to see this one task to fruition. In fact, it would be accurate to say that he was the antithesis of what safe suburbia offered and represented. It was an anathema to him. Getting married, buying a starter home, having kids, his and hers matching bathrobes, going down to the local pub for Sunday lunch, inviting people — other couples, of course – around for dinner parties, cutting the grass on the weekend and washing his car; all of this would have resulted in a numbing of his spirit and consigned him to a lingering premature death. His mind would experience this fate long before his body. He was a rebel, but not without a clue.

He upped the speed slightly to mirror that of his increasing excitement. This was better than any line of cocaine he had ever taken. It was more erotic than any blow job he'd received. It was stronger than any moralistic resolve he had ever had. He was mesmerised; he was charmed; he was smitten. Attacks of morality aside, he enjoyed and derived great pride from what he did, but he had never experienced this level of euphoria. It was consuming. It was powerful, but stopped short of being overpowering. He couldn't stop smiling. He upped the speed again just slightly and turned off the high street.

The planning and execution was always meticulous. It was orchestrated with precision and nothing was left to chance. That said, there was always an element of the unknown or unforeseen coming into any scenario. These occupational hazards, due to this planning, were minimised, and, if the unforeseen did happen, there was always a back-up plan.

The targets were never less then three hours' driving time away from the lock up. Nothing was locally sourced and a time delay of an hour was factored in, in the event that the owner encountered his own set of unforeseen circumstances.

Baskin was a seasoned professional and knew the pitfalls. Due to his ambition to scale the heights of the underworld hierarchy, his work rate and planning were ambitious, but, nonetheless, achieved. He instilled this discipline in his protégées. He saw himself as a benign philanthropist. His protégées made him money and his remuneration was generous. He slept well at night.

* * *

Jez drove calmly through the Hertfordshire countryside in a two-year-old Mini Cooper. Not all Baskin's clients were wealthy. Most were, but some were average social climbers embarking upon a mission to scale the heights of what they imagined constituted success.

The spec of the car. The body work, whether it was trendy and the latest motorised must-have; all these were irrelevant to Jez. This was merely a job to him. Albeit a job he was good at. In fact, a job he excelled at. Being good at a job and deriving job satisfaction don't necessarily go hand in hand. This certainly was the case with Jez. It was all about remuneration. That was all the motivation he needed.

He seldom asked questions. He just let Beanmonkey divide the list up, and off he went.

He turned onto the M10 in the direction of London and the direction that would signal the end of today's job. He couldn't wait to hand over his car, take his money, and then go somewhere and get drunk. He was bored. In fact, he'd been bored for quite a while. He'd become so bored of the same routine. Although he was able to separate enjoyment of what he did from the pragmatism of simply getting paid, he was, nonetheless, getting weary of doing the same thing week in, week out. It's accurate to say that most people, unless involved in a job that they consider to be a vocation, find the monotony of routine irritating. Jez, however, always reached a point in everything he did where monotony eventually triumphed over financial pragmatism, and he tried another area of employment.

Yes, he was feeling now that he wanted to do something else, or perhaps even do nothing for a very long time while he considered his options. He didn't want to do it alone, though. He had grown very close to Beanmonkey and wanted to maintain some sort of continuity. They had, from time to time, discussed leaving the life they were in and trying something new, but it was never a serious consideration. It was generally a conversation conducted under the influence of alcohol only to be dismissed the next morning. This time, however, it felt different. There was no reason why they couldn't just jump ship. They would, of course, have to plan this, and it went without saying that they would keep all plans secret. Plus they would, of course, have to leave London. However, this wasn't a problem. Just like work, Jez got tired of being in the same place too long. London, just like car theft, had been nothing more than an experience to him, and it had run its course. When he was bored, he moved on. It was the same with everything he did or experienced. Girlfriends came and went. Places were swapped. Jobs were abandoned and changed. Interests were changed and some circumstances rekindled. He was constantly evolving. He didn't know how to be static. Perhaps one day he'd learn this. It was unlikely. He was relaxed, but restless. He was inspired by life, yet equally weary of it. The only constants in his life were his friends. He loved his friends. His friends loved him. They were his lifeblood and, apart from money, shaped his life. This was why he had been so willing to help Miles. Miles felt relieved at the prospect of having someone with such an infamous reputation to help him through his turmoil and to guide him through the streets of London, but what Miles didn't know and was beautifully oblivious to was that Jez wasn't doing so reluctantly. He was in fact embracing what he viewed as a very welcome respite from what was again becoming a monotonous existence. Helping Miles through his turmoil would take him – albeit briefly – away from this path of boredom and empower him once again. What he hadn't allowed for, however, was the effect Miles' arrival would have on him. Something had changed in Jez and it was all down to Miles' arrival. Perhaps it was the contrast of innocence with the abandonment of it. The naivety of Miles' innocence and, in particular, his pronouncements in the Swan a few days back, had taken Jez by surprise and had taken root in his mind.

* * *

The tiramisu had been very much to Baskin's liking, as had the smoked salmon on wheaten bread and the veal scallops for the main course. The wine had been well chosen and her choice of table décor had been inspired. Natasha had done well. Baskin was proud of her. He smiled up at her and nodded in approval. She smiled back. All this made Baskin look good in the eyes of his more cultured guests. Everything he did or had done for him had an ulterior motive.

Mr. and Mrs. Johan Bildecker had also enjoyed the meal. They liked coming around to the Baskin residence. They found their earthy, *nouveau riche* take on life fascinating. They also found it mildly amusing. They found it amusing that people believed they could buy class if they had the right amount of money. Others, of course, in the circle of which the Baskins were also a part of, didn't quite view it in the same light, but, like the Bildeckers, went along with the charade.

The Baskins were, of course, oblivious to all this. Jimmy wore the finest suits. They were all designer, of course. Armani; Boss; Hilfiger; Pravda; Fellini. He even had some suits custom made in Saville Row. Natasha drove a Porsche Boxter, had numerous Gucci handbags and an endless supply of designer shoes, which, had she been still alive, would make Imelda Marcos green with envy. Money was everything. It could buy you anything and it could influence anyone.

Jimmy sat back in his deep leather reclining seat with a smug and self-satisfied grin etched onto his weathered face. Not only had he enjoyed a most superb dinner party, he'd beaten Johan Bildecker at Backgammon. This had never happened before and the shocked expression written across Bildeckers face as he left the house bore this out.

From the first throw of the dice to the bearing of his first checker, he knew that victory and the spoils thereof would be his. The spoils weren't much, but, again, to Baskin, it was what they represented. He didn't like losing. Not in the way most people dislike losing; it was more that he was obsessed with winning. He'd only taken up Backgammon two months prior to this glorious night. Bildecker, on the other hand, had been playing it for years.

The last time Baskin had lost against him, he had taken it particularly badly, literally not speaking for days. He hated that feeling so much that he had vowed revenge. So, for the next two weeks, when he'd return from work, he'd go straight into his study and immerse himself in all things Backgammon, and tonight all those lonely nights and mental toil had paid off.

Natasha went over to him and kissed him on his forehead. She was proud of him.

"I'll leave you to bask in your glory, darling. I'll see you upstairs in a bit."

Baskin nodded and smiled back in recognition. Nothing in his life had come close to the high he was now feeling. Not even buying his first – legally acquired – car at just eighteen. Not even sending his oldest to Harrow. Not even buying his three-year-old a pony, marrying Natasha or even buying his current home. No cocaine he had ever taken could have achieved this high. This was an ego-induced high of huge proportions. He felt on top of not just his world, but the world, full stop. He'd stay exactly where he was right now and bask in his moment of victory. It had, indeed, been a successful night.

5

Danny Hall

Jez had just heard about the fate of Danny Hall. Danny, a work colleague and, to a slightly lesser extent, a friend of two years who had fallen prey to Baskin's displeasure, was now lying in Northwick Park Hospital. He had undergone a most severe beating. It was unclear as to exactly what the circumstances that had led to this were, but, as Jez knew, one didn't have to fall too far from Baskin's grace to enact his wrath. From time to time, he had heard of other misfortunate fellow employees who had suffered the same fate, but, as he hadn't known them personally, the impact had been mostly negligible.

This time, however, it was completely different. It was shocking and very unnerving. Danny wasn't just another statistic to Jez, and, although he wasn't as close to him as he was to Beanmonkey, he was someone Jez considered a friend. They'd been for drinks together. They'd been to see QPR play. They'd been around each others' homes. They'd laughed together and they had had a laugh together. Jez and Beanmonkey had both been present at the birth of his son, Nathan, and, swept up in the enormity of it all, had both cried. Slightly expected of Beanmonkey; largely unexpected of Jez. All said, Danny was now lying in a hospital bed, most likely nursing severe injuries. Jez was slightly uneasy visiting him, lest Baskin found out and viewed it – as wouldn't be beyond the realms of fantasy – as some form of disloyalty. However, if that scenario did arise, the worst he could expect would be a stern talking to. It was still a rather scary prospect, though. That said, there was no way he wouldn't be visiting Danny. He owed him that much.

Unfortunately for Jez, Miles had been present when he had received the call. This posed a dilemma for Jez. It was a dilemma he could have done without. He was having a difficult enough time trying to process what had happened to Danny. He could easily do without the scenario whereby Miles saw, in black and white, a harrowing component and striking realisation of the very life Jez was in. Miles' innocence had impacted on Jez to the extent that he wanted to shield him from the possible end results of such a vocational choice. Due to the naive moralistic energy flowing from Miles, Jez felt uncomfortable and, for the first time, an imposter in his own lifestyle.

"So, because he was late delivering a car, he was given a good kicking?" asked Miles, trying his best to take it all in.

"That's it, Milesy. It doesn't take much for him to do this kind of thing. I really think that the bloke's unhinged."

"You don't say," said Miles in mock surprise. "Really?"

"Yeah, yeah. I know. Anyway, I'm going to see Danny and I'm going alone. I don't want you too see this."

"To see what?" asked Miles

"What da'ya think?" asked Jez. "To see this life we're mixed up in, of course. Most of the time, the job's all right. I get into the car and off I go. But then this happens."

"I'm a naïve little twat, Jez, and even I know that it's a possibility that can happen at any time. I don't know why you're so surprised."

"I'm not surprised. Just a bit in shock. It's Danny Hall. He 's a mate."

"Anyway, you can't leave me here alone here," said Miles. "I take it he's been here before? What if he shows up and finds me here? You can't really take the risk if he's as mad as you say he is. I don't know why don't you go to the police."

"Yeah. You're right, Miles. It's better if you come. But what else can I do? I suppose I could go to the police station and tell them I'm in the employ of a certain James Walter Baskin, prominent underworld boss, and I have it on good authority; he's put a mate of mine, who is also employed by him in hospital. Get real, man."

* * *

Danny really was in a bad way. The X-rays had revealed that he had a fractured skull, four cracked ribs and a fractured cheek bone. He had also had to endure being kicked in his genitals a number of times. The pain from this being so severe, forcing him to pass out, had subsided somewhat, but not disappeared.

Psychotic he may well have been. Perhaps also sociopathic, but Baskin wasn't stupid. There was method in his brutality. Each time he meted out punishment to his employees, it was, indeed, brutal, but it was never enough to put them in mortal danger. After all, they were his friends, but, more importantly, they were important assets to him. Every driver he employed had to undergo what he called auditions. These auditions, which were carried out on a disused air strip near Uxbridge, involved various tests. In mock exercises, the applicant was given the task of breaking into a car and driving it off at speed to a hanger on this airfield, where they'd be met by Frankie. They were marked on speed, technique and dexterity. Generally around half of those recommended to Baskin met with his approval. The rest were thanked for their time and driven back home. So, whilst carrying out what he viewed as justified retribution, it wasn't in his best interests to punish them to the extent that they'd be out of action for a long period. There was a constant supply of replacements waiting in the wings to fill in while the objects of this retribution convalesced. That said, Baskin didn't like his young charges being out for too long, so the punishment was never too severe. This time, however, he'd overstepped the mark somewhat and he knew it. He felt bad.

He was finding it difficult to concentrate. Upon reflection, this beating hadn't really been merited. Yes, the delivery had been late, but this hadn't caused any adverse knock-on effect. After all, he'd only been half an hour late and the person picking the Jag up from the lock up, due to being stuck in traffic, which, in turn, had been caused by an accident, had phoned ahead explaining that he'd be an hour late. The delivery to Bermondsey docks had been made on time and the car was now en route to Bahrain. An unnecessary beating had been carried out and now Baskin was worried. He knew the back-up driver, Pete Stamp, was a capable replacement, but he rated Danny his best and most reliable driver, apart from, of course, Beanmonkey. Anyway, it was done now and Baskin had to find a way to relax. This was essential. He had to do the roses. He needed to. He'd get Franky to take him.

'Doing the roses' was yet another manifestation of Baskin's disturbed and damaged mind. Granted, no acts of violence and rape were involved, but it was still disturbing. 'Doing the roses' involved going to the rose garden in Barham Park. He'd walk through it smiling for the whole duration. If he didn't feel like smiling, he'd make himself smile. He also imposed upon himself a rule which meant that thoughts pertaining to violence, lust, dishonesty and general wickedness were banished throughout this brief sojourn. This was his happy place.

Frankie would drop him off, then wait for him for the duration. It was usually five minutes, but no longer than ten. Frankie, one of the few people privy to his rape sessions, found the 'doing the roses' thing even more disturbing.

*   *   *

Jez and Miles were sitting by the bedside of Danny in intensive care. Miles was silent. He was transfixed. He'd seen the result of people who had a beating inflicted upon them before, but he'd never seen anything like this. This was wrong. It was pure, unabashed brutality. One side of his face was swollen. It was a bluish and pinkish raised blob. It really was disturbing Miles. He shook his head and got up.

"Jez, mate," he whispered. "This is really freaking me out. Is it okay if I grab some air?"

"Of course, mate. Go for it," replied Jez.

Miles walked towards the exit, and Jez looked blankly at Danny. Danny, having been sedated, was out. Danny was a big man. He was one of those people who had a presence about him. It wasn't all down to his physicality; it was, in equal part, down to his charismatic refrain. People generally liked him and, if they didn't, there was something lacking in these people; perhaps a sort of underdeveloped persona. I mean, how could you not like someone like Danny? Whilst it is a clichéd and often lazily dispatched statement, it was, in all honesty, very accurate to describe Danny as a nice person. He was simply that. Apart from his occupation, his life was very basic. It was simple and it was uncomplicated. He provided his family with a good, comfortable life. Not just financially, but emotionally. If he didn't know someone, he'd always give them the benefit of the doubt. He tended not to pre-judge people. His life was a small, neat circle comprising his little boy, his girlfriend and his friends. Like Beanmonkey, he wrestled with his conscience from time to time. He liked being decent. He liked decent people, but he knew what he was doing was decidedly indecent. It didn't stop him, though. Now here he was a physical wreck with wires all over him piercing his tattooed arms. This gentle giant had been reduced to a feeble and physically redundant shadow.

* * *

Baskin stepped outside Barham Park. He felt revitalised. He felt invigorated. He felt rejuvenated. He felt somewhat, though not completely, absolved. However, clarity of thought, which the roses had handed him, allowed him to evaluate what had happened and what penance, if any, would have to be carried out. After some deep soul searching, he had decided to forgive himself. He had, after all, acted wholly in haste. There had been nothing premeditated about what happened. Yes, he had been brutal, but it wasn't brutality that he had enjoyed dispensing. He had done it with a heavy heart. That said, Danny himself had played his part. He knew – everyone knew – that Baskin's pet hate was a late delivery. In fact, that sense of punctuality wasn't just confined to business dealing; it extended to all areas of his life. Although he refrained from handing out beatings to those who turned up late to social gatherings, as he didn't think he had the right to do so. The work environment, however, was a different story. That said, he realised that he had overstepped the mark. However, it was fine, as he'd forgiven himself and he'd bring Danny a few grand. He'd see him right.

* * *

Miles was beginning to wonder what he'd got himself mixed up in. Putting up with Craig's bullish rants and overbearing presence was nothing compared to what he'd just seen. Although, he had hit his mother and he couldn't be allowed to get away with that. That was a given. He wondered what kind of person or people could be capable of inflicting such pain and damage on another human being, and what, if anything, justified doing it. He was in with the big boys now and he knew it. He'd have to make a plan. He could, of course, go home. This was no life to be caught up in. It was no life at all. Yes, they had plenty of money, but what happened to Danny could so easily happen to Jez and Beanmonkey, and it could happen at any time.

All things considered, I think I've made my point now. There'll be no shame in going back. I showed that I wasn't afraid of Craig by twatting him, and with his own wok! I've made a difference to Mum's life by doing that. Craig will never try that shit again and, after what I've seen, sharing a house with that twat will be a piece of piss. But if I leave now, will I be running away? I mean, I don't have to get caught up in this line of work. I can't even drive, so he'll have no use for me. And with Mum putting money in my account every month, I'll be fine for cash. If it gets too much for me, I'll go away for a few days until I feel all right.

* * *

Although Jez exterior displayed a nonchalance that stated that he tended to let events drift over him, it wasn't the full picture. He did have an ability to take a practical and, to some, a perceived rational logical approach, which sometimes bordered on apathy, but he wasn't impervious to those around him or situations such as this. What he was seeing now was affecting him deeply. He had been

somewhat detached from the previous beatings he had
heard of, as he didn't really know the victims. He had heard
of them by name, but didn't actually know them. Therefore,
he was able to maintain an emotional distance. This,
however, was completely different. Unlike Beanmonkey,
Miles' naively dispatched opinion about what they do being
tragic had had a negligible affect on him. He couldn't now
help dwelling on them, as he looked closely at Danny.

Jez had been late on four occasions delivering to
Baskin. On one occasion, he'd turned up nearly an hour
late. Granted, it hadn't been his fault, but Baskin never saw
it like that. He'd wondered how and why he'd managed to
escape the fate handed to Danny.

*This could be me lying here. Shit. It could be me. I
guess it's all down to luck, really. I guess it depends what
mood the big man's in at the time. I'll just have to make
sure that I'm never late again. If I stick to that, I'll be safe.
He'll have no excuse. But he doesn't need an excuse. I'll
just have to play this safe. No drinking the night before and
an early night. Yeah, if I stick to that, I'll be safe. I'll go
over and see Suze after this. God knows how she's feeling,
poor dear.*

* * *

Miles walked back in through the hospital reception. He
had more or less made up his mind about deciding to leave.
It was all very well getting swept up in what he considered
to be dangerous glamour, but witnessing the end product of
this lifestyle had proved very sobering. Whatever life in
Carlisle was, it wasn't even remotely as challenging as the
one he was now observing. Anyway, he'd made his point
and it had had a positive effect on all involved. He could
now return with his head held high and without the threat of
recrimination hanging over him. There could be no

recriminations. In fact, he could see himself being welcomed home with open arms; well, by his mum, anyway. Craig would, at worst, be a benign force brandishing nothing but a redundant, intimidating grimace, and, at best, perhaps the potential to be a changed man, someone who had been shown the error of his ways by a skinny sixteen-year-old.

* * *

Natasha Baskin pulled up to the riding stables. She was really excited. She'd wanted to have a go on Daisy for weeks now, and today she was getting her chance. As a child, she had always felt jealous of the posh kids who went riding on the weekends. She had always wished that she could have been one of them. Now, thanks to her husband, she could go riding whenever she wanted. She could buy shoes, expensive handbags, jewellery, dresses – designer, of course – nice perfume and the most up-to-date and desired fashion. She could holiday in the South of France, although they seldom did. She could get up when she pleased and take a dip in their swimming pool. She was a member of a golf club and, because she was a lady of leisure, could go whenever she pleased. Because she had so much time on her hands, she had honed her skills so much to the extent that she was now actually better than her husband, although she never displayed this when they played each other. Her husband always won. She liked it that way. Anything else, well, that would be plain disrespectful. She liked him to think he was in charge at all times. It suited her.

She trusted him, but doubts as to exactly what he did to keep them in this lifestyle were beginning to appear. In all their time together, she had never seen where he directed his import-export agency from. Every time she asked to be brought along, he had an excuse. They all seemed plausible at the time. She had also not seen any of the artefacts' he sold. One would imagine that any proud business man would want to show off his possessions, and, with Baskin being arrogant, one would expect him to be a prime candidate for such elaborate displays of grandeur. The truth was, yes, Natasha did like the fact, as she believed it to be, that their lifestyle was down to the importing and exporting of fine art. She was, of course, a social climber, an unabashed beacon of social ascension. She would have liked what it represented. However, if she had found out that it was, in fact, due to car theft, whilst being initially disappointed, she would not have asked him to cease doing it and get a normal job. That was not even a remote possibility. She had the lifestyle that she had always craved, and the reason she had it was down to money. It was all fuelled by money, and getting money was the most important thing. Yes, there would be better ways to get it, but, if pushed, she would easily choose luxury through ill-got gains over just getting by doing an honest day's work.

She got out of her car and walked over to the stables. She was brimming with happiness. It was going to be a good day. She could feel it.

* * *

Jez, Miles, Danny Hall and Baskin, by contrast, weren't having a good day. The rejuvenation and absolution Baskin had felt after his jaunt in the roses had subsided somewhat and he was now worried. He was worried that the beating would come back to haunt him. It would be more accurate to say that perhaps he still felt absolved from guilt, but was worried about the possible consequences of his actions. Pete Stamp had done a good audition. Baskin had been impressed by the dexterity shown, but this was a big job for a novice. His client, Monsieur Paz Bacanda, was one of his most valuable. Over the years, he'd been a steady client, putting at least half a million his way. He had yet to let him down, and to do so would represent a fatal mistake. Usually, he'd start the 'freshies' – his name for those who had successfully completed the audition – off on less lucrative jobs, jobs that, if they did go wrong, would have a minimal effect on his business. This time, however, he had little, in fact, no choice but to put his trust in the hands of a freshie. In all probability, he knew the likelihood was that all would go according to plan. It had to.

* * *

Jez gave Suze a tight and lingering embrace. She was crying and Jez was doing all he could to prevent himself from following suit. He never allowed himself that indulgence in public, and especially now, not in front of Miles. After all, he had set himself up as his mentor and had a duty to see that through, no matter how long that took.

"Thanks so much for coming around, Jez, and for bringing your wee friend around, too," said Suze in her soft Glaswegian tone.

Miles, although irritated by her description of him as 'wee', maintained his sympathetic refrain. "It's really nice to meet you, too, Suze," he said. "I just wish it was under happier circumstances."

"Me too, Miles. I don't know why, but there's something calming about you. I can't quite put my finger on it. Anyway, don't mind me. I'm just prattling on, as usual."

Miles smiled and nodded.

"Anyway, Suze," said Jez, whose voice, by now, was showing emotion. "You take care, pet."

He went over and hugged her again. He felt that he didn't want to let go, as he could feel himself liable to break down at any stage. Suze pulled away and smiled.

"Look, let's try not to worry." she said. "He's a mountain of man. He'll be fine; sure he'll be home in no time. Although, hopefully not back into this ridiculous mess."

'This ridiculous mess' she was referring to was, of course, the line of business they were in. The fact that they as a family derived great financial stability from this business had never been enough to offset both the shame and the fear she felt each time he went 'off to work'. Like a policeman's wife operating in the most intense and dangerous environment, she never knew in what state he'd return that night or if he'd come back at all.

She looked on as Jez and Miles walked down the driveway. Miles' whole presence and general demeanour had had a strangely calming effect on her. It wasn't what he had said. Yes, he had mentioned that he felt uneasy that 'his best friend' was involved in such work, but it was the humility and the objective calm in his voice when doing so. She had found it incredibly moving.

This just isn't worth it anymore. It never was, but especially not now. She turned and walked back into the comfort of her warm house.

* * *

Whenever Jez voiced his intention or, moreover, his desire, to draw a line under or write a new chapter in his life, the aspirations were short lived. They usually started to dissipate shortly after awakening the next morning to the residue of the alcohol, which had fuelled this thought process. This time, alcohol hadn't formed part of the equation, but pain had. Nastiness had. A complete lack of empathy to one's fellow man had. Anger, evil, distain, hatred, sadism and an overwhelming display of mean spiritedness had. It was unjust, cruel, destructive, self-destructive, demeaning, and self-demeaning. This time, something would have to give. This time, something would have to change. Fast and seamless dissipation wouldn't be coming into the equation this time.

A weary and exhausted Jez extinguished his cigarette and relaxed in his bed.

6

Frankie Peterson

Frankie was an awesome sight. He was the typical quintessential hard man. He stood at six feet, eight inches. He was a skinhead, had a face like the proverbial bulldog and a ridiculously overdeveloped body, which suggested that he was seldom out of the gym. His association with Baskin went back over five years. Before Baskin had diversified into the 'second hand' car business, his main concern had been debt collecting. He was only too willing to hand over sums of cash to the needy in various council estates in West London and even more willing to collect the vastly inflated interest. Invariably, due to circumstances beyond their control, some found it difficult to keep up with the repayments. This is where Frankie came in. All it took, generally, was one visit. In most cases, when people saw him, they'd capitulate immediately and somehow find the money. It probably meant their family going hungry for a week and consequently having to borrow again to survive. Of course, Baskin again would only be too willing to oblige. It was a perfectly crafted vicious circle. As little or no outlay of energy was required, this was an easy little number for Frankie. That said, due to the lack of physical contact, it did get boring sometimes, so, to alleviate the boredom, he'd sometimes give them a kicking all the same.

He was really excited. He hadn't debt collected in a long time. He'd missed it. Although he was a loyal and unswerving servant to Baskin, he'd taken serious issue with him over the demise of the lending side of the business. Despite having had a steady stream of potential customers, Baskin had neglected it, preferring instead to concentrate on his import-export wing. This had always been a bone of contention with Frankie. He liked debt collecting. He especially liked it when things didn't go according to plan. Most of the time, people had the money ready and the correct amount. This was a huge source of irritation and disappointment to him, as he enjoyed flexing his muscles and seeing the fear on the faces of the customers. It empowered him. His call to action was akin to that of a trained soldier longing for a war.

Frankie, due to his size and general demeanour, stood out. He wasn't your average person who could simply blend in and become part of the crowd, except perhaps at a BNP rally.

He stepped up inside the cab of his four-wheel drive 'Dodge'.This extra-large car provided the perfect and wholly appropriate vehicle for a man of such stature and standing. He felt proud driving around in it. Whenever he drove into an estate, he'd herald his arrival by pressing the horn. It made a trumpeted tone, signalling his intent. It was a sound that struck fear into his intended victims. They knew when he'd be visiting, as he always gave them advance warning. He was kind like that. That said, no matter how much notice they had been given, it never acted as much of a cushion in absorbing the fear and, in some cases, terror they felt when he came to visit.

When it came to dishing out punishment, he didn't discriminate. The clientele was a broad church comprising pensioners of both genders, single mothers, unemployed, students and others from less obvious social groupings.

He'd be only too happy to hand over the requested amount of cash. This he did with exemplary politeness. His voice was warm and slightly audible, and he nodded and smiled when handing it over. He loved playing the social philanthropist only to lull them into a false sense of security. This worked beautifully and proved very profitable. If the first payment or, for that matter, any subsequent payments, were defaulted on, the initial loan spiralled into something so large that it bore no resemblance to the original amount. The whole business was designed in such a way that people couldn't help but default. This would then result in the recipient being lumbered with an impossible dept to pay off and being in financial bondage. Consequently, a continuous supply of clients was assured.

Much to Frankie's annoyance, when deciding to sink his efforts in his car venture, Baskin had decided to offer an amnesty of sorts to those indebted to him. This involved having to pay reasonable and achievable sums in order to clear their accounts. Now that he had found what he considered to be his vocation, he wanted to be rid of all distractions. The vast majority jumped at this guilt-edged opportunity and delivered; some, however, didn't quite make it. People like Glen Johnston.

Glen was unemployed and dabbled in petty crime. The type of crime he was engaged in was so petty that it was a matter of opinion whether it was perhaps slightly pedantic to classify it as such. There was never any violence involved and no vast sums, or, for that matter, significant sums of cash changed hands. Glen was a junkie and lived in a council flat squat with two other junkies. The petty crime, which was used to pay for his habit, involved the movement of copper. Copper piping mainly and copper stripped from church roofs. He generally got by in terms of having just about enough to fund his habit. Sometimes he had a little left over. He had been forced into approaching Baskin as times, for a short period had seen lean pickings. The onset of the recession had resulted in less buildings being built, which, in turn, had resulted in far fewer building sites furnished with copper piping. Most churches had dispensed with copper roofing, opting instead for a more modern and cheaper felt finish. So, a combination of hard times and a lack of ambition to diversify helped push him into the arms of Baskin. Baskin hated junkies. He hated what he termed the 'sad demise of society'. He blamed the whole breakdown of society and its subsequent dispensing of decent values on drugs. Squalor, degradation and disease were also in his mind down to the tacit acceptance of drug use. Yes, Baskin hated junkies, but then again, he'd lend to anyone.

Although he knew Frankie was coming, he was surprisingly calm. He didn't feel at all frightened. He had the cash and, as soon as he handed it over to him, he'd never have to see him again. He knew Frankie was dangerous with a propensity for gratuitous violence, but it wasn't bothering him. It may have been something to do with the fact that it was only two hours since he'd had his last hit and he felt nice and relaxed. In fact, he was looking forward to being able to hand the money over and finally draw a line under his dependency on credit. Just like drugs, there are good credit sources and ones that could potentially cause damage or, even worse, kill. This was definitely the latter.

This will all be gone soon. I don't know why I'm not even a bit freaked out about him coming. He scares me, usually, but I'm not scared right now. He'll be here, then he'll be gone. It's that simple. It's that sweet. He'll be finally gone. That meathead parasite. I know I'm a junkie, but I'm not the one who preys on the needy. I nick copper from churches. I nick copper piping from building sites. Big deal. They can afford it. Churches are rich and so are construction companies. People like to say me and my kind are scum. Maybe we are, but at least we don't attack people. People who do that. Now, they're the real scum.

Frankie trumpeting his arrival into the Bellshouse flats complex and drove up to the entrance to Greenfield's house. He loved coming here. Looking around at the general squalor and urban decay added to his inflated sense of self-worth. Each unwitting inhalation of stale urine from the stairwells compounded this illusion. This was another reason he was glad to be back; he'd missed it. As a rule, he showed such deference to Baskin; it bordered on sycophantic. He had no problem doing this, as, outside Baskin's remit, there were plenty of other areas in which to assert his own elevated status. His size and general reputation handed him 'alpha male' status among established friends and those he was introduced to. His reputation preceded him. It was largely a case of Chinese whispers. His reputation did precede him, but, by the time the stories of his perceived greatness and influence had filtered down towards the end of the line, it had been distorted beyond all belief. He didn't mind that, though. It suited him.

He was now approaching Number 55 Greenfield's House. The door was open and Glen was leaning confidently against it clutching a yellow folder. He looked completely relaxed. This was making Frankie uneasy. It was also attacking his position as the harbinger of fear and intimidation. Why was this? Usually, people were terrified when meeting Frankie and their facial expressions reflected this. Glen was no different. Overcome with fear of what lay ahead of him, he had even broken down and cried on one occasion. This time, it was different. His relaxed demeanour clearly expressed not just a confidence in himself, but a total disinterest in whatever intimidation

Frankie had to offer. He was even smiling. This wasn't just making Frankie uneasy; it was annoying him.

Why's he smiling? He doesn't even look scared. What's his fucking problem? That's not the way it's supposed to be. What a sad little tosser.

Glen looked straight, head on, at Frankie.

He certainly doesn't look the big man today. Does he? Maybe he's been out of it all for too long.

Glen outstretched his arm and handed the envelope over to Frankie. "There ya go, big man. Count it if you like. But I'm sure you'll find it's all there."

Giving him a blank, dismissive look, Frankie took the money from him and began counting it.

"It's all there, Mr. Frankie. Yeah," said Glen mockingly. "Well. It is, isn't it?"

Frankie nodded in agreement. "Yeah. It's all there."

"Well then, big man. That concludes our business. Be lucky, mate. Tarahh."

With a mocking, almost confrontational grin, Glen stretched out his hand to shake Frankie's. Frankie slowly returned the favour and the two hands met. Glen, fixing a confident gaze on Frankie, started moving his hands in a downward motion. Frankie looked down. He couldn't bear to look Glen in the eye. He felt ashamed. He felt embarrassed. He felt down. He felt broken and he felt defeated. His world had come crashing down upon him and, with it, his sense of dominance. It wasn't supposed to have happened this way. The hunter had had his poison removed and it had been done so with stealth-like precision. Yes, Baskin was the proprietor of this venture, but Frankie was the real boss. The poor frightened souls were splattered upon his canvas of urban decay, and his tools of intimidation and intense physicality employed to great effect. Baskin gave him the slips of paper, but it was Frankie who orchestrated events in his own chosen manner.

This was his world and he alone decided how events unfolded. It was different this time. Something had changed. Today, events had been dictated back to him and he himself was now the object of derision, of ridicule and of dejection.

Defeated and with his world imploding, he turned and walked back towards the stairwell. As he started his assent, a stench of stale urine wafted up toward him. He wretched. He looked around him, the reality of the squalor becoming increasingly apparent. This, putrid stench no longer heralded arrival onto his stage of conquest. It was the stench of defeat and underlined what was singularly, the only significant and ultimately successful attack on his bullish dominance

* * *

Miles couldn't relax. He couldn't get the image of Danny Hall out of his mind. Just lying there, unconscious and with all those wires sticking out of him. He'd never seen anything like that before. The feeling of being out of his depth was increasing with the passing of each hour. He sat in the flat looking aimlessly out of the window. The view was, at best, uninspiring and, at worst, depressing. Having the great *Radiohead Bends* album playing in the background wasn't helping the situation, either. He walked over to the CD player and looked for something that may help to lift the mood or perhaps even level it out. He couldn't see anything. He turned off the music and slumped into the sofa.

What kind of person could do that someone? What type of world has Jez got himself mixed up in? Has no one ever even tried to break away from this life? It's hardly a life, really. They may have money, but they're really slaves. Jez probably thinks that it's just another line of work. It's not.

What's the worst thing that can happen if you screw up in a regular job? You get a disciplinary. You certainly wouldn't end up in hospital! And that was for a late delivery of a car. What if he didn't even manage to get the car in the first place? What would happen then? What? Would he kill him? He's my mate. Surely one day his luck will betray him and he'll miss out. What'll happen then, and he said he's been late delivering, too. It's only a matter of time before something bad happens. When I think of it, it was nothing like this back home, but then that's one of the reasons I left home.

* * *

Jez had just left Northwick Park and was walking towards up towards Harrow on the Hill. Although Danny was still in a bad way and indications had shown that he'd most likely be in for a further two weeks, he had regained consciousness. This was a huge relief for all concerned. For his family, his friends and the hospital staff, because, although they didn't know him personally, they weren't impervious to other peoples' grief. It wasn't like most jobs where one could detach association from their jobs from personal emotion. This was deeper. This, after all, was the caring profession. It was about the tragedy of someone so young being in such a precarious situation. From the first moment his head had been laid on the off-white pillow in intensive care, the unspoken good wishes and aspirations were out there in the public domain. Amongst the staff attending to him, a film of good wishes and aspirations of hope hung in the air over his bed. Even Baskin got in on the act by sending a bouquet, which, ironically, read 'Wishing you a speedy recovery and a peaceful stay. All our love, Jimmy and Tasha'.

Although Jez liked Miles and quite enjoyed having him around, he desperately needed his own space right now. Beanmonkey had said that he would be in and out of the house most of the day and, if Baskin did show up when he wasn't in, Miles was under strict instructions not to answer the door. The margin of error was so slight that Jez felt relaxed enough to be able to leave Miles in the flat and head up to see Danny alone.

He'd noticed that Jane and their little boy had visited earlier, as, among the various 'get well' cards, was one from his loving 'fruitee' and 'bannanaboy'; the pet names for Jane and their son, Josh. He'd probably just missed them. Jez knew the potential pitfalls of the game he was in. The threat of police prosecution was a constant. All it took was one wrong turn or even a slight hesitation and he'd be in trouble. Baskin, of course, had always said that in that event, they were to deny all association. They would, of course, comply. There was nothing to be gained except perhaps a reduced sentence and, more importantly, they were too afraid not to. Again, he'd heard of those who had fallen foul to Baskin's strict set of rules, but the impact on him had been largely negligible. He didn't really know them and it was their own fault; at least, that what Baskin had said. However, this was different. He had been shocked when hearing about Danny's fate, but it was worse when seeing him first hand. He felt numb. He felt cold. He felt scared. He felt as if there was nothing he could do to stem what he now viewed as a malignant force. He felt angry, so much so that if his senses, for one moment, had taken leave of him, he could quite easily have gone up to Baskin, pointed a gun at him and pulled the trigger. That would have been the easy part. The hard part would have been the aftermath. This aftermath when the shield of blind rage had disappeared and he'd have to deal with the consequences. It didn't bear thinking about. Baskin knew a lot of people, with his influence extending far beyond West London.

He took the large Vodka and Redbull in his hand. This would the first of many tonight.

* * *

Frankie was sitting in his favourite chair. It was such due to a few factors. It was leather, very wide, and had it was a La-Z-Boy recliner. Whenever he had had a bad day or just generally if things didn't go according to plan, he'd head home, roll himself a big spliff and plonk himself down in his La-Z-Boy. With the effects of skunk weed meandering through his bloodstream and slumped into his La-Z-Boy, he was back to himself within minutes. This time, however, it was different. He couldn't expel his feelings of dejection and an overwhelming sense of failure. His whole approach today had been quite impotent and facile. Yes, he'd received the payment and Baskin would be happy. Baskin didn't care how he got the payment as long as he got it. What methods were used to get it were irrelevant to him. The problem was that they weren't irrelevant to Frankie. The collection of monies owed was secondary to him. It was how he performed in getting the money that was the important thing. It was all about the performance and, today, he had by his own strict standards performed well below par and it was eating away at him.

He's only a weedy little junkie and I bottled it. A fucking scanky, pot-faced diseased piece of shit. I'm Frankie Peterson, for fuck sake. Frankie fucking Peterson. I'm someone and he's nothing. Ah shit, man. Or maybe it's 'cos I aint done it for a while and I'm a bit rusty. I'm gutted, though. He wasn't scared and that's the bottom line. He really got the measure of me today and he knew it. That's the problem. That skinny fucking junkie cunt got the

measure of me and I let 'em. There's no fucking excuse for
that, Frankie boy, no fucking excuse.

He wasn't handling this well. Here was this big,
muscled, scary, hard man who'd come up against a weedy
junky and felt wasted himself. He'd felt small. He'd felt
insignificant. He'd felt worthless. This was horrible to him.
It wasn't how he viewed himself. It certainly wasn't how
others viewed him. He was feared, and for good reason,
too. After all, he was Frankie. He didn't care if he was
liked. He had a choice to make between being liked and
being feared. Both, to him, were mutually exclusive. So, he
chose the latter. The latter suited him. It was what made
him who he was. It was what defined him. It was the very
essence of what made him who he was. The complete
person he wanted to be. Okay, not everyone had the choice
or was fortunate enough to be able to be in a position to
affect choice. Identity, for most, is something that purely is.
It's a static sense of being. Frankie was static. He didn't
change organically, but he did affect it. He liked being a
hard man. It was important to him.

He was trying to tell himself that this feeling of
desolation would eventually pass, that it would run its
course, but he was struggling to visualise this end game.
Right now, he quite envied Baskin, as he had a way of
dealing with such feelings of foreboding. After all, he had
the roses. Granted, it was rather disturbing, but at least he
had something that worked, and it was original. Frankie, on
the other hand, had no way of processing such situations, as
he'd never had to before. He was thinking, perhaps, of
going out, getting drunk and securing a fight. The only
thing was, this time, as his confidence was at an all-time
low, he wasn't sure if he would reign supreme. This was a
strange and unwelcome new feeling, which he would have
to process and expel. He'd have to. Baskin was very astute
and he'd sense something wasn't quite right, and there was

no way Frankie could lie. Baskin would know that he was lying, and he'd warned Frankie never to lie to him and that, if he did, he'd be severely reprimanded. There was no way he'd lie. It wasn't an option. He'd have to deal with it.

* * *

Jez had done a great deal of his own particular processing. Many hostelries had been visited and a great many measures of Vodka and Redbull consumed. In truth, he hadn't really processed the events of a few days; he'd merely numbed the pain, but that was needed. In a few days' time, he'd be back behind the wheel of someone else's pride and joy en route to Alperton. That was what he did and it was, in large, part of who he was. Pragmatism was now returning to his mindset. He couldn't and would never be prepared to make sense of what happened to Danny. That was senseless and somewhat unbelievable. It was also inconceivable that such a fate could befall someone simply for delivering a car half an hour late. This, to Jez, was ludicrous, devoid of justice and logic, and an attack on morality. He hated Baskin right now, but he was shrewd enough to never broach the subject in his presence. That in itself would be a declaration of suicide. He'd bite his tongue and continue to deliver. He'd continue to deliver for the foreseeable future, but, right now, he couldn't see himself doing it indefinitely. Miles' arrival had, indeed, heralded – subconsciously in Jez and consciously in Beanmonkey – a suggestion of possible change. It was almost as if he was some self-proclaimed messenger.

It's a nice idea, but that's all it is, really. We can't just up and leave. I mean, where will we go? Thailand? Yeah, right. That's just a dream, too. We'll never go there. I mean, what would we do? We don't even speak the language. Then again, there's plenty of Brits over there who can't, either. It's just that I'm getting tired doing the same thing all the time, and then Dan. How could that happen to a friend of mine? But then, what else can I do. I'm brill at what I do and the pay's mint. But I'm still a slave. This proves it. I've got to decide if I'd prefer to be free and poor or a rich slave. Maybe the boss will let me go when the current list is completed. All he can do is say no. But then what if I ask him and he flips? That could well happen. He's a fucking loon.

* * *

The principal of fair play is one that, in the ideal world, should be given unbending observance. The landed class and their associates tend to abide by this rule. The *nouveau riche* has its own rules governing this. It's by no means a society based on liberty and equality, but it is very much based on fraternity. This was why Baskin, regardless of how much money he managed to amass, how many top of the range cars he managed to accumulate or how many riding lessons he sent his wife on, would never be a part of this fraternity. Quite simply, he didn't fulfil the criteria. His treatment of Danny was a prime example of this. It was unwarranted. It was unjust and, more importantly, it was vulgar. Aspiration and hard work alone would never secure him entry into this elusive fraternity. His accent was wrong. His clothing, although expensive and of good quality, was too showy, and the fact that he liked to mention how much the particular article of clothing he was wearing cost, or who the designer was, merely underlined this gulf in class. His wife was too common. Her attempt at trying to effect what she would term 'a posh accent' served only to underline this, her perma tan and bleached hair punctuating this fact. He may well win at Backgammon, Chess, Billiards and excel at clay pigeon shooting. He may well, through tacit retention of memory, remember and be able to name poignant pieces of music from Chopin to Vivaldi, but that wouldn't make him any different to a trained parrot. The truth was, this man would be at best feared, but liked by very few and never respected by those whose respect and acceptance he craved. At least, though, he'd always have 'the roses'.

7

London Calling

There was something about street entertainers that both intrigued and annoyed Miles. On one hand, they provided a welcome respite for the foot-sore traveller, but, on the other, they played the guilt card with aplomb if you dared walk away after their performance without first showing your appreciation on a monetary level. Miles, being of a sensitive disposition, wasn't impervious to such attacks and, more often than not, found himself digging deep in order to avoid feeling guilty.

This particular busker Miles was intrigued by was a potential basket case. He was about seventy years of age and was standing awkwardly in a pair of scuffed shoes, which had come apart at the seams. Behind him lay a cheap tape recorder playing a compilation of assorted songs. Attached to his left hand was a lead, and attached to this lead was a flea-ridden spider monkey. The act itself consisted of a foot tap and dance routine. While the old man tapped his foot, he gradually unravelled more of the lead, allowing the little monkey, which was dressed in a red waist coat and matching fez, to dance around. Two important issues now occupied Miles' thoughts: care in the community and issues of animal cruelty.

What kind of society could throw a lunatic like this back on to the streets, in order to save on the costs of looking after him? And how did such a loon manage to get his hands on a spider monkey? To do that, you would need an exotic pet license, and to get that you'd have to be in a position from which to wield some sort of influence. A footballer, perhaps, or maybe a pop star, but a full on loon? How is this been possible?

A strong waft of onions from a nearby burger cart hung tantalisingly in the air. He looked at both performers again. He had seen enough. Was his motivation for watching this borne out of a need to be entertained or from a strange fascination with the macabre? Either way, the lure of a salmonella-infested offering was proving too strong. He made his way towards the burger van.

It seemed to him as if everyone had descended upon Leicester Square. The place was absolutely buzzing. Buzzing with the sound of buskers, buzzing with the sound of feet pounding the pavements, buzzing with the hum of traffic all mixed in with a strong sense of urgency. Apart from the Baskin incident, he was enjoying his time in London. Even Wembley and Sudbury, which he had initially disliked, felt different from anywhere he'd previously seen. They felt as if they were part of something bigger, something more important. It was quite often said that London is made up of thousands of urban villages which surround its heart, a curtain raiser to the main event; the scene setter. There exists among most Londoners a certain sense of detachment from the rest of the country. A sense of aloofness, but not from the standpoint of arrogance; more based on a sense of pity that the rest of the country is lagging so far behind and 'there is nothing that can be done about this'. It's British, yet very English, very English, yet very different. Of course, with Miles not being a Londoner, he wasn't cursed with the full extent of this infectious aloofness, but he was beginning to understand its nature.

Within this hive of activity, he felt a sense of calm. In fact, this heightened activity was helping to take his mind off the events of the previous days. He wasn't sure if going into central London under the current climate may have been viewed as somewhat insensitive. As Jez and Beanmonkey were both out doing what they did best, it wasn't an issue. Moreover, it was the current climate that had acted as the catalyst for the journey. He'd also felt the need to re-establish his original view of London. The view that he'd held before the inconvenience of reality had had the nerve to show up. This sense of calm was helping to lay the foundation for a sense of excitement. A sense of excitement at being in the centre of his own representation of what London was. Of what London should be. After all, there really was no point in going to and living in a place where the highlight of the day is to go to a chavvie little local and get a kebab on the way home. He could do that in Carlisle. No, coming to London was supposed to be a dynamic experience, an experience that, by the time he felt ready to return home, would have greatly enhanced him. He was enjoying this journey into his own vision of logic. It also felt good to be able to immerse himself in this fantasy. With the correct image now returning and fully ensconced among the other players, he continued his journey down towards Whitehall.

* * *

Beanmonkey, needing to purge himself of guilt, yet again, was back at St. Jerome's carrying out the obligatory penance. Despite this circle of events being repeated for nearly two years, it never got easier. It was only during his chat with Arthur that he could feel the self-loathing slowly drain away. Each time at the beginning of his journey of penitence, such was his overpowering sense of guilt that he always found it difficult to visualise when it would all fall away. History, of course, should not only have told him that it would, but also when it would. Perhaps it was the contrast of what Arthur represented and espoused against the immoral practice Beanmonkey was engaged in. Putting his life on the line for others, as opposed to taking from others; going out of his way to help his fellow man, as opposed to being a hindrance in his fellow man's pursuit of joy. Putting others first. Without being conceited, Beanmonkey knew that he had the capacity to be more like Arthur and less like Baskin. Actually, he was nothing like Baskin, but, by moving in the same circles as him, he was, by association, similar. He had to get out and perhaps he would take Arthur up on his kind offer sooner rather than later. The problem would be convincing Jez. Jez always spoke of doing something else, but, after a while, it became obvious to Beanmonkey that extended procrastination would reign supreme. Even Beanmokey himself never gave such suggestions serious consideration beyond a couple of days' child-like enthusiasm. The fate of Danny, though, was challenging this short sightedness. He would sit with Jez later and have a serious discussion, and put Arthur's proposal to him. Arthur had a cottage in St. Ives, Cornwall. Arthur's suggestion was that they go to this cottage and treat it as a break, and use it as somewhere from which to regroup. Also being the romantic and poet, he thought that the serenity of St. Ives would provide the perfect contrast between the polluted lives they led. He hoped that, free from all manner of pollution, their clear minds would facilitate entry into a more moralistic arena.

After emptying numerous bed pans, mediating yet again in disputes over what was watched on the communal television and carrying out the obligatory clean up of vomit, he was now in Arthur's room on the final leg of his penance.

"For what? A half hour? It shouldn't happen at all, but half an hour. What kind of man does this? What kind of man is this? Actually, I know what kind of man this is. I fought against men like him in the war. I fought against everything these brutes stood for. I tell ya, Anton, if it wasn't for the fact that you were mixed up with him, I'd dob 'em in. Have you given any thought to my offer?"

"I'll be honest, Art. When you put it to me, I gave it serious consideration. I was mesmerised by the idea, actually, then, well, ya know, you get caught up in things and next thing you know, it's kinda lost its importance."

"Well, consider it again. How long can you continue doing this? Don't get me wrong, lad, it's nice having you come to visit, but it would be nice if you didn't need to steal cars in order to do it. You really need to consider it."

"I know, Arthur. Of course you're right. It's just that after a while you feel yourself drifting back into your usual ways. Basically, life takes over and you're back to square one. Although, nothing like this has happened before. Well, at least not this close to home, anyway."

"The way I see it," said Arthur, "you have a choice to make. If you carry on the way you are, you'll always be looking over your shoulder and you'll always be coming here seeking absolution. Oh, incidentally, consider yourself absolved. But yes, what do you want to do? Do you want to remain a slave? You have a choice."

Those words were having quite a profound effect on Beanmonkey. He'd never heard the word 'slave' used to describe the part he played in his chosen profession. He was also in a semi state of shock at the previous events and was now feeling that, contrary to what Arthur was saying regarding having a choice in all this, he didn't, in fact, have any choice; he had to leave. As he was otherwise engaged and their paths hadn't crossed much, he hadn't really had much of a chance to sit with Jez and discuss it, but he had seen a look on his face that he'd never seen before. It was a look that screamed 'I can't process this; I haven't a clue what to do'. It was a look that shouted 'I'm beyond terrified'. It was as if he was just alive, but without any of the hallmarks of life. He was just a shell. If he was going to put Arthur's suggestion to him, it may be a good time to do it. He liked the idea of the contrast between their current London life and their possible, albeit temporary, relocation to St. Ives. The way he now saw it was that, rightly or wrongly, they had quite a bit of money saved. Between them, they had about thirty thousand, so they could take as much time out as they wanted to decide their next move.

* * *

Sitting behind the wheel of a three-litre, fuel-injected, chrome-coloured, sleek Alpha Romeo 166, Jez was operating on auto pilot. He had decided that the beating of Danny was the catalyst that perhaps he had subconsciously been seeking. He was now sick of the control Baskin exerted on all those around him. Prior to Danny's attack and, to a lesser extent, Miles' arrival, he'd been able to conveniently push the reality of what he was involved in to the side. He didn't seem to care either way. He just saw this control as a fact of life. All he had to do was uphold his end of the deal, then he'd receive his reward. He didn't care if he liked Baskin or not. Yes, it was still there in the background and, on some occasions, it would rear its ugly head in the form of an attack of conscience, but it was always swiftly and rather easily dealt with. He was now also beyond afraid. This was good, as he found it easier to wander through to the next goal; that goal being complete liberation from Baskin. Up until now, he'd felt indifferent to Baskin. If the jobs were completed without hindrance, then Baskin was usually a benign force. The reality of who exactly he was had been known, but the realisation of it was easy to ignore. This had now changed and it could no longer be ignored. Prior to all this, the only person Jez and, in reality, all his fellow scrumpers, intensely disliked, was Frankie. Frankie lacked the subtlety of Baskin in how he dealt with people. He was clumsy, oafish, crude intimidating and unnerving. At least Baskin made an attempt to hide his dark side; Frankie made no such attempt. He was an open book. Jez had his own way of displaying the lack of respect he felt towards him. It was in his swagger when delivering his target. It was the glint in his eye and the wry smile he displayed when handing over the keys. Frankie never gave up trying to intimidate him. He had this almost hypnotically terrifying stare. It scared most people, but Jez always made sure to never avert his gaze. Everything about him screamed out in no uncertain terms that he wasn't in any way afraid of him or impressed by his overbearing stature. Frankie's whole *raison d'êtres* of intimidation was highly successful on most, but rendered impotent when it came to Jez. He'd seen Frankie the previous night, leaving Northwick Park Hospital after visiting Danny. Again, he'd given him that stare and again Jez had stood his ground. Only this time, there had been something different about it. It was as if Frankie was just going through the motions. In fact, he looked uneasy. It was as if he was getting into character just for the sake of it. Although Jez always stood his ground in his dealings with Frankie, it was usually done so under a feeling of foreboding. His own private feelings of foreboding, which he usually kept from Frankie, weren't even in existence this time. Perhaps it was due to the circumstances of the previous days and operating on auto pilot, but he couldn't help but feel that there was something weaker about Frankie. He couldn't quite put his finger on it. If he wasn't so preoccupied, he may have even gone in for the kill.

Due to the circumstances of the last few days, he hadn't had much time to gauge how Beanmonkey was feeling. He wasn't sure how he'd take the news of his finally leaving it all behind.

Maybe he'll be surprised, but I doubt it. He's never seen me in such a state before. I'll leave even if he doesn't want to leave. It'll be a bit weird starting all over again, but it's about time I did. I can't understand people like Baskin. He didn't have to do that at all. There really was no need. Anyone outside what we do must wonder why we do it. I don't think money's enough anymore. Its other people's cars and we just take 'em. What does that say about me, though? It's taken a mate of mine to get a kicking for me to realise that what I do is wrong? That's wrong itself. It's completely wrong.

* * *

Baskin opened the drawer and pulled out a near-full bottle of gin.

"Are you sure about what you saw? I mean, completely sure? You couldn't be mistaken, could you? Jeremy knows how I feel about drugs. Everyone does."

"I'm afraid so, boss," said Frankie. "He'd come out of the bog with the stuff over his nose; a bit careless, if you ask me. And not only that, he then walked over to a geezer and shook his hand. Only, it wasn't as innocent as it looked. Before the other geezer could close his hand, I could see, quite plainly, a wrap. What a silly boy, Mr. Baskin, so not only is he doing drugs, it looks like he's dealing, too."

"I mean, he knows how I feel about that filth. Why would he do this to me? It's not right, Frankie, and I'll be telling him that."

Jez was now coming up to Park Royal. He was now taking a somewhat philosophical view of the situation. He knew that what he had been engaged in for the last few years was wrong on a few different levels, but he wouldn't be doing this anymore. He was still young enough to make mistakes, but old enough to learn from them.

He had to take a pragmatic approach to it all. There was no other option, really. He'd lived in a moralistic void for a few years, but he'd gained financially. *It's as if I can hand money back. It's done now. All I can do now is move on. I'm not proud of what I've done, but it's done now. I have to move on. I need to move on.*

Like a marathon runner who drags up a reserve of energy for the final leg, he pulled into the estate at speed. This was nothing more than a personal gesture, as he was on time. *At least I won't be getting a kicking,* he thought. Outside the lockup, he could make out the overbearing frame of Frankie. *I'm going to enjoy winding him up,* he thought. *Especially seeing as it is for the last time. I'll make it special!* He pulled up to a smirking Frankie.

What's he smiling for? He's a bit more upbeat today. He wound his window down. "Oh, Frankie. You okay, mate? You looked a bit off colour yesterday."

"Of course, mate," he replied. "Good work, Jez. Very good work. Mr. Baskin will be well pleased."

Jez was somewhat taken aback. Frankie had never been so normal in his discourse towards him. He'd never called him by his name before. He got out of the car and, as was custom, gave Frankie the keys. Usually, he handed them to him. This time, he threw them to him. Frankie caught them and smiled.

"Thanks, Jez. I'll take it from here," said Frankie, grinning.

Jez walked in through the slightly open steel shutter. Baskin was standing there, dressed, as usual, in his tasteless crombie. This was a sight that he wasn't going to miss. Baskin looked at his watch.

He shook his head in a gesture of approval. "Well done, Jeremy. You're on time. Come in. Have a drink."

This is weird, thought Jez. *He's never done this before. What's going on here?* He followed Baskin into his office. Standing beside Baskin were two men. Two big men. Two men sporting menacing smirks. He had no idea who they were. He tried quickly to recall ever seeing them. He couldn't. *Why are they here*, he thought. *And why is Baskin inviting me into his office for a drink? He never does this. Something's not quite right here.*

Still sporting a smirk, the more rotund of the two walked over to him. A swift, unexpected punch to his waist brought Jez swiftly to the ground. He coughed and looked up in terror at Baskin. Baskin was laughing. Another kick came crashing into his ribs. Thoughts of foreboding came flooding into his mind. He was terrified beyond belief. He wanted to speak. He tried to blurt out words, any words. Words that could say, 'please, stop. Why are you doing this', but none came out. He looked around and up into the face of Baskin. He couldn't understand why it was happening. A second kick crashed hard into his ribs. This time, he screeched out and recoiled in pain. Thoughts of terror were overpowering him.

"Okay, okay, that's enough. That's enough," said Baskin. Baskin stood over him and leant downwards. There were tears in his eyes. "Drugs? Drugs, Jeremy?" he exclaimed loudly. "You were good. You were very good. Not as good as Anton, mind, but good all the same. I'll never forget the day of your audition. You turned up brimming with confidence. You had that glint in your eye. You looked so full of manly purpose. Diya know what I mean? I said to meself, 'you know what, Jimmy, you've got a good one here. He'll do well'. Then I watched. I watched as you confidently strolled up to the motor, stuck you knife in the side of the window, jumped in, fiddled around for a bit, then off you went. Poetic, it was. You then drove off into the sun. It was perfect. It was flawless. I said to myself, 'there's something special about that boy'. And then this drugs. Drugs? And you know how I feel about that filth. It's poison. What would me old mum think, Jeremy, my darling old mum? She was so proud of me, ya know, but she wouldn't be now." He pointed up to a picture of his mother, which hung just above the fan light. "I'm disappointed, to say the least."

Frankie walked in holding a bag containing white powder. He placed it on the table. "I'm afraid this confirms it, boss. It's a sorry day, indeed."

"But I aint been dealing drugs. It's not mine," said Jez. "He's planted it on me. He's always had it in for me. And you know why? It's 'cos I aint afraid of him and he knows it. Can you not see that? Please, Mr. Baskin."

Baskin nodded over to the second and taller of the two strangers, who nodded back and walked over to Jez. Jez, fearing another outbreak of violence, covered his face with his arms.

"Oh, Jeremy. There's no need for this. The pain's over now. I think you've learnt your lesson," said Baskin.

The man helped Jez to his feet and walked him over to a chair at Baskin's desk. He helped Jez sit.

Thoughts of Danny lying in the hospital bed, helpless and with wires attached to his arms, came flooding back to him. He feared that it wasn't over and that there was much worse to come.

Sitting opposite him and with the bag in his hand, Baskin shook his head. "Jeremy, Jeremy, for a start, relax. Nothing more is going to happen to you. I'm thinking of Danny. Last week, I acted wholly in haste and I've regretted it ever since. I mean, I trust Frankie, usually, but I should also trust my own instinct."

"But, boss," said Frankie. "You've got the evidence in your hands. What more do you need?"

"Ah, Frankie, Frankie, always the loyal servant. All I'm saying is that I should perhaps have done a bit of my own investigation. I have to say that it's all worked out very well, what with all the evidence falling into my lap like this. How very fortunate. Don't you think, gentleman?" He looked towards the two strangers. "Do me a favour; would one of you gents take young Jeremy here home?"

The more rotund of the two helped Jez up and walked towards the door.

As the man helped Jez towards the office door, Baskin stood. "Again, Jeremy, I'm sorry for acting in haste. I really should think things through in a more calm and measured manner. I'll see you right, son. You can count on that. I'll be in touch."

Jez, forcing a smile, nodded back. Out of the corner of his eye, he could see Frankie. He looked at him, still maintaining his grin. Frankie looked uneasy and his left leg was moving almost involuntarily.

Baskin turned to a rather disturbed-looking Frankie. "Right then, Frankie," he said. "A wise old man once said, 'all that glitters is not gold'. Do you know what that means? No? Well, let me enlighten you."

8

The Lockup

This was foolhardy even by Miles' standards. Talk about going in to lair of the dragon itself. This was madness and suicidal, but he didn't care. So driven was he by what had happened to Jez and hungry for answers that he was willing to put himself in harm's way. He was completely single minded and was being driven by an anger the scale of which he'd never before felt. It was beyond anger. It was fury, and it was this fury and a strong desire to acquire justice that was adding momentum. Rational people in the same situation would be scared. Miles wasn't. A certain amount of fear is healthy, as it allows one to take stock and assess a given situation. It's a survival mechanism. It's in the DNA. It's all about self-preservation. All traces of rationale had deserted him. When Jez had arrived back in the state he had, Miles could barely speak. This was strange for him, as the opposite was usually the case. He could see by the fact that Jez was conscious and able to speak that it wasn't that serious an assault and could potentially have been a lot worse. However, the effect that this had upon him was quite marked. His face was devoid of any emotion. This was a cause of concern for both Jez and Beanmonkey, as the normal, even healthy, thing to do would be to react in some way. Apart from uttering 'oh my God' when he had seen Jez, he had stood speechless and stolid for five minutes. It was as if he was in deep shock. Again, Jez couldn't help feeling guilty for having agreed to invite him into his world. He knew that it wouldn't take long for his own wounds to heal, but could help thinking that Miles' healing process may take that little bit longer. Jez hugged him in an attempt to elicit some form of emotional release, but to no avail. They thought that not only was it odd, it wasn't healthy for him to be so devoid of words or emotion at a time like this. He then looked at them with seemingly lifeless eyes, hugged Jez tightly, then went into his room. They hadn't seen him since.

He waited for Baskin and two thickset heavies to get into a car. He sneaked in behind a wall just as the car passed. This lockup-come-warehouse was exactly as Beanmonkey had described. It was dreary and, in Miles' mind, in need of a good lick of paint. It was architecturally and industrially imposing. Not in a good way, like, for example, Battersea power station. Listed building status on Battersea power station wasn't just appropriate; it was essential. This place, with its top two slightly cracked small windows, its massive yellow shutter gates and its faded red brick, was every bit as ugly as Beanmonkey had naively described to Miles. He had thought that Miles was just being curious, not that he'd actually break in to the place.

Look at this place. So this is where my mates work. They must be so proud.

He walked up to the front of the building. He could just about manage to get in through one of the small windows, but the chances were that someone would see him. He had no idea how long Baskin and his entourage would be, so he had to act quickly if he was to gather whatever information he was looking for. The building was standalone. He decided to check around the back and the sides in the hope that there was some way in. He walked down the left side. It was all brickwork and, even if he did manage to scale the walls, getting in through the roof was too dangerous a risk to take. He went around to the back. There was a door, but again, no windows. Again, he toyed with the idea of going in through the roof.

Nah. It's not worth the risk. Knowing my luck, I'd fall all that way down and not die instantly. I'd be writhing around in agony until Baskin and his uglies got back and God knows what would happen then.

He walked over to the right side. Again, there were no windows. His only hope now was to see if he could kick in the fire escape.

I'm a skinny wee shit. Like it's going to work. Fuck it. I've got to at least try. Apart from a foot and a shoulder, I've nothing to loose, I guess.

He went back around and went over to the door. He tugged at it to test its resistance. Then, to his delight, the door swung open.

Fuck sake! That was easy! What a stroke of luck. The tools forgot to check it! Haha!

He pulled it slowly shut behind him and walked in quietly. The place smelt of petrol. It was even more imposing from the inside. It somehow looked bigger. In the middle of the building were some pulleys extended from the ceiling and a sunken rectangular area in the ground. Two tables stood either side of this area and were adorned with all manner of tools necessary for the ID changing of some poor soul's pride and joy.

For some reason, Miles wasn't at all fazed by the fact that he was in the centre of the lair. The place was exactly as he'd imagined. He was finding the stench of paint fumes a little over powering. He looked around again to see if he could spot the office.

There has to be an office somewhere. I doubt if Baskin does his admin at home.

He walked towards the top of the building. As he got closer, he could pick up on a stench of stale urine.

Well, at least I know where the toilets are now. He walked past the toilet. There was a door just past it. He pulled the handle down. Again, to his amazement and joy, it wasn't locked. He walked in.

So this is the nerve centre of the operation, he thought. *This is where fortunes are made and lives destroyed. Right, I need to act quickly.*

He went over to the desk and began looking through the paperwork, which was strewn across it. *Nah, nothing. Just receipts for shopping. There's lunch receipts. Oh, and here's one for a Porsche. Fuck me, 40K!* He then proceeded to the drawers. He looked in the first one. It was empty. The second one. Empty. He then tried to open the third one, but it was locked. *Shit! This is obviously locked for a very good reason.* He looked frantically around on the desk, but there were only papers and a few pens. *Think, Miles, think. There must be some way to get in. Ah, that's it. I'll have a look at the tools. I'll see if I can smash it open.*

He made his way over to the tables. He looked at the first one. *Brilliant! A hammer. Yes!* He looked again. Most of these tools, he hadn't seen before. Then, to his continued joy, he saw it. Sitting there in all its glory was a screwdriver. *That'll do nicely.* He grabbed it and ran back in an enhanced state of excitement and wonder. The adrenalin was pumping through him with ferocious speed. He wedged the screwdriver in the drawer and began hitting it with the hammer and with unbridled enthusiasm and strength, which he hadn't thought he possessed. After many attempts, a gap began to appear at the top. There was now just enough of a gap to be able to fit the whole screwdriver in. He put the screwdriver in and pushed. The drawer swung open. To his amazement, there was a gun and a bundle of photographs. He stood in shock. He felt sick.

This was a complete eye opener. He stood rooted to the spot, motionless. He gagged, but stopped short of vomiting. He picked the top photograph up. He could barely look. Curiosity got the better of him. He took a closer look. He couldn't believe what depravity he was seeing. He was in shock. *Oh my God. This is sick. It's wrong; it's disgusting.*

As well as being controlling, violent, delusional, psychotic and plain nasty, Baskin was a voyeur. He liked or, rather, insisted upon, watching some of his employees having sex with random women they'd met in Baskin's reserved VIP areas, in certain London nightclubs. When it came to other women, he practiced uncompromising fidelity. He was loyal, you see. Having sex with other men, wasn't, in his mind, cheating. That was different. It was rape. So, after some heavy petting, Baskin would be invited to join the lovely couple in their hotel room and indulge in a spot of voyeurism. He really got off on watching other people enjoy themselves in this way, but he also sometimes liked being watched, and, in some cases, even photographed.

Miles looked closely at the photograph. Tears were now beginning to form. He was shaking. The picture showed Baskin behind what can only be described as a male victim. He was pulling his head back whilst brutalising him. It was dark. It was evil. It was also sad. It looked as if this victim was screaming, perhaps even pleading. There were tears in his eyes.

Oh, my God. This is just wrong. It's evil. It's wrong. Why? Why is he doing this? Why can't he go somewhere and pick someone up? Like a bar? He doesn't need to do this.

I've got the bastard, though. I've fucking got him. He needs to be punished for this and for Jez and for Danny. He needs to be punished for messing up people's lives. It needs to be done. Why has no one done anything before? He'll pay, though. He'll certainly pay. I can make him pay. I've got him now!

He gathered his thoughts and the photographs, and picked up the gun. He put the gun and photographs into his holdall, and made his way towards the fire exit.

* * *

Things were improving for Jez. He was now sitting up in his bed. The pain had subsided somewhat and the doctor had visited. No broken bones or any injuries of significance had been sustained; just bruising and minor pain was the diagnosis. He'd realised just what a lucky escape he'd had, but also realised that it wasn't safe to stay around. It was now obvious that Baskin was not only a vicious thug, but he was a vicious thug with mental issues.

Beanmonkey was standing by his bedside.

"Trust me, mate. Do you really want to stick around here after this? First Danny, now this. He's out of control. He don't know what he's doing. Okay, you got off lightly. Well, compared to Danny, you did. But what if he hadn't had a change of heart or if no area of doubt had crept into his mind? You were lucky. You could be lying in hospital too, beside Danny in intensive care. Or worse, mate."

"Beans, you're preaching to the converted, mate. We need to get out, not just today, but we need to get out now. What if he changes his mind again? We need to get away quick. Where's Miles?"

"I don't know. He left about an hour ago. He didn't say where he was going. He was just sitting there in stony silence. I think this has really got to him. Anyway, I'll phone him and we can meet him somewhere. The main thing is to get out as soon as possible. I'll call a cab."

Although not personally responsible for attacking and injuring himself, Jez couldn't help but feel a bit guilty at the effect all this had had on Miles. Granted, he didn't have the benefit of a crystal ball and, therefore, could never have predicted the series of events of the last few days, but he still felt responsible.

I'd no idea where all this would end. I'm more worried for him than for me. Although I'm leaving it all behind, it's still a world I'm used to. I've always lived, to some extent, on the edge. He hasn't. He's soft as shite. He's an innocent lad. He'll never be the same again. This'll all have changed him. I hope it hasn't. Miles's is canny. I don't want him to change. I wish I'd never agreed to put him up. If he loses who he is, it's down to me.

* * *

Miles was walking up Sudbury High Street. He looked at his phone and noticed that Beanmonkey had called; twice. He didn't care. He was preoccupied. He was walking with such purpose. He wanted to do something. He felt that he had to. At the outset, he hadn't known what he was looking for and what he would do if he found it. He certainly hadn't expected to find what he had. He now felt compelled to act. He still felt sick. He had this strange taste at the back of his throat, which had been induced by the sickening images he'd seen. He'd vomited a couple of times and was on the edge of repeating this at any time. Yes, he had wanted to lose his innocence. Well, he'd well and truly lost it now. There really was no going back. He wasn't the same person anymore. He was no longer the naive little boy-man who had left Carlisle in such a rush. He'd wanted to lose the innocence, but not in a way where it threatened to change his whole character. All he'd really wanted to do was toughen up a bit and visit places outside the confines of his little world in Carlisle. He felt sad at such a violent passing of his innocence. He blamed Baskin. This would have to be processed. Action would have to be taken. He'd lost himself. He'd lost who he was. He didn't feel as if he had anything to lose. He was angry. He was furious, not just at what had happened to Jez, but now at the loss of his innocence. This was all down to Baskin and who he was as a human being. He had imposed himself upon his friends and, in so doing, had imposed himself and his cancerous effect upon Miles. Miles was infected. Baskin had infected him and there was no going back. Baskin would be dealt with.

It's all changed now. It's changed completely. I feel numb, but I also feel angry. How can that be? That makes no sense at all. Something will have to be done. I'll do what I have to. I'll do what I want to. I'll do what I want to him and how I want to do it to him. I don't care about his family or what affect it's gonna have on them. It's not my fault. I'm angry, but dead inside. If I'm dead already, I've got nothing to fear. Fuck him for doing this to me. Fuck him and fuck his madness. I don't care what happens to me now and what I do as long as I do him. After all, I'm dead. What more can happen now?

He walked with purpose into the Swan and up to the bar. Ian, the camp kiwi, was serving.

Miles nodded. "Half a Stella and a double voddie and coke, please, Ian."

"Are you okay, sweetie?" asked a concerned Ian. "You look a bit off colour. Perhaps a coffee would be more in order."

Miles was taking Ian's concern and manner to be some sort of flirtatious behaviour. He was, of course, wrong. Ian was a good-natured and caring person who was genuinely concerned. He was a sensitive soul who sensed that all was not right in the world of Miles and was merely expressing this.

Still, as Miles' thinking and his emotion were off colour, he saw it as flirting. In light of the material that he had sitting in his bag, this was making him feel very uneasy.

Since he was old enough to understand what they meant, he had hated people conforming to perceived ideas of stereotypes, but, all throughout his life, he had been confronted by them. His local shop owner was Asian. The builders whose services his father had employed to build his extension were all Irish. The owner of Guilio's, his local Italian barbers, had a foul temper. Every fat person he had ever met was jolly and laughed too much, and now here he was being served alcohol and flirted with by a big, fat, mincing bearded queen. He wasn't in the mood for this. He wanted to say something. He felt almost compelled to do so. In light of what had transpired and what he was holding in his bag, the last thing he needed to do was to draw any attention to himself. Also, he was finding it increasingly difficult to process what he'd seen. He wouldn't be best placed to challenge Ian on what he considered to be in bad taste. He was a long way from being in the correct frame of mind to mount any form of reasonable discourse. *I'm only sixteen and he knows I'm underage to drink here. The fucked-up, queer bastard. If he knew what I had in my bag. Those sick, messed-up images. Those unnatural images. Those images of rape. Of a man getting raped. Okay, he doesn't know. But he still shouldn't be trying to gay me up. It's better if I say nothing. I'll lose it. I'll blow it.*

"I'll be fine with the beer and voddie, thanks, Ian," he said, maintaining a calm exterior.

He waited patiently or, at least, that's the impression he tried to give off. He felt sick. He felt dirty. He felt violated in some way. He felt unclean. He felt tainted and he felt damaged. He was worried that something central to his very being, the very essence of what defined him, had been damaged, possibly beyond repair. He was beginning to wonder if he'd done the right thing. When he had broken in, he hadn't known what he was looking for and what he'd find. It was the kind of scenario that whatever it was he was looking for, he'd know when he found it. Now that he had it, he didn't know what to do with it, and, if he did nothing, he had damaged himself for no gain at all to anyone. Even if there was to be a gain. *Is this really worth it*, he wondered.

He took his drinks and headed to the unpopulated areas close to the pool table. He could sense that Ian was very aware that something wasn't quite right. He needed to avoid eye contact. He'd steady himself with a drink and sit, and try to process events.

Oh, my God. What have I done? This is way too big for me. Maybe I should tell the lads and let them decide what to do? Fuck it, I can't, though. If they know, they'll be involved and that's not fair considering they didn't ask me to do this. They've got enough to think about. They certainly don't need this. No, I'll just have to deal with it myself. This Baskin bloke is evil and something needs to be done. But by me? Little soft as shite Miles Goodwin! Fuck! I've done it now!

Despite being in the thick of such a dire and potentially terrifying scenario as this or, moreover, because of it, he let out a little chuckle. The irony of a small, timid, middle-class wet-behind-the-ears boy like Miles taking on one of the most feared men in West London was ringing clear to him. He laughed again; this time, it was more of a full-on, high-pitched one. This was good and it was very welcome. Good, because it took the heat off him somewhat in that any concern Ian had for him would be allayed and welcome, because, while he was being amused, he wasn't in the depths of fear. Fear with little snippets of laugher and amusement seemed the order of the day, so it seemed sensible to make the most of these respites.

Indeed. Never look a gift horse in the mouth, he thought. Again, he laughed, but, this time, there was a sound of desperation in it.

Ian looked over. "You okay, little guy?" he asked.

The fact that he had even asked this annoyed Miles. *Why doesn't he just mind his own bastard business? And little guy thing again. I'm five point four; that's not little, anyway. Why do people call me that?*

"I'm fine, thanks, Ian," he said. "Just something I remembered."

Ian nodded and smiled.

I hate this situation. I don't know what to do. I don't know what to feel. Well, I know how I feel and I don't feel good. This isn't right. This is nothing compared to Craig. The stupid macho Irish fool has nothing on Baskin and his pricks. I've got to do something, but what?

He was heading towards despair now, somewhere between catatonia and terror. He could feel words and sounds bouncing off the inside of his head. He suddenly felt nauseous again.

Ah, come on, Milesy, not again. Please don't. Control yourself. You have to. Please don't. Ah, come on, please.

As he tried to control the inevitable, tears started to trickle down his face. He began to sob. He didn't care who saw him now or what they had to say.

Ian had known all along that something wasn't quite right with Miles. He'd known from the moment he had seen him walk in. He'd had his head down, slumped. He was avoiding eye contact and Ian was curious as to why this was.

A good bar person isn't just someone who pours drinks beautifully and with panache. A good bar person is also one who can multitask in a number of different disciplines. He generally displays analytical skills comparable to those of a seasoned psychologist. Such is his power of recall that he can provide impartial and highly effective mediation in bar disputes. He can show empathy when called upon to do so and can dispense justice when forced to do so. He commands respect without needing to ask for it and elicits warmth and friendliness, and his powers of observation are unrivalled.

Without hesitation, he came swiftly from behind the bar and over to Miles. He hugged him. Miles sank his head into Ian's shoulder and continued to sob.

"Look, matey," said Ian. "I'm not even going to ask you what's on your mind. It's your business and I'll respect that. But know this, sweetie, I'm here if you ever need to talk or a shoulder to lean on, or even cry on. If you want to tell me, you know where I am."

Miles looked up with tear-stained eyes. The beginning of a crescent-shaped smile was forming.

"Ian, I so want to tell you, but I can't. I've lost it, though. I'll tell you that much. I wanted to lose it, but only if I got something back in return. I haven't, though. It didn't happen the way I wanted it to. I've lost it and now I want it back. But I know that I can't ever get it back." He put his head firmly back into Ian's tear-soaked shoulder.

Ian increased the embrace.

"Mate, whatever you think you've lost, you'll probably find that you haven't actually lost it, but mislaid it somewhere. We all wish for things that we haven't got, only to finally get them and realise that they weren't really that important after all. But none of that means that you can't take a trip back to what you had before. I'm sure you'll find it again. You just need to remember where you last had it, if that makes sense. Does that make sense, matey?"

Miles lifted his head and looked up at Ian. His eyes were now bloodshot, but his crescent smile had reached full maturity.

"Actually, no. It makes no sense at all," he blurted. "But thanks all the same for helping me smile."

9

Ben Stillcome

Natasha assembled the flowers together in a nice neat bundle. There was an assortment of her favourites. This neat bundle included lilacs, orchids, geraniums, and roses – white, of course. She liked the symbolism; to her, it represented beauty and untainted purity. There were also blue crocuses, all topped off nicely with a daffodil. She remembered that he liked daffodils. She wasn't sure if this was due to his Welsh lineage. Although he'd been little older than two when adopted, he had never forgotten where it had all began for him. His adoptive parents had never felt the need to erase it from his mind. It was important for them to give him the complete picture. There was no crisis of identity for him. To him, his parents had been the ones who had fed, clothed, loved and nurtured him. The ones who he had lost touch with, the ones who had made him; both were important chronological aspects of his life. From time to time, he had reminisced about a life that he neither remembered nor really experienced. He liked to reminisce. He needed to reminisce. It gave him his feeling of *hiraeth*, the longing for his sense of 'home'.

Without meaning to state the obvious, funerals are, by definition, sombre events. In most cases, it's usually expected, to some degree. The person in question has reached a certain milestone and, although a sad event, it's usually acknowledged that he or she has had good innings. In other cases, the person has been suffering from an illness so, when the inevitable does happen, the blow is softened somewhat in that it has been expected. This death, however, represented neither scenario. Nothing had prepared Natasha for this. She was holding up well, though, surprisingly so.

With the flowers now prepared, she fixed her black shawl into place over her shoulders and went out to wait for her lift to the funeral home. She had to be strong for the sake of Jasmine, her three-year-old. Fortunately, she was at that age where the full impact of what had happened wouldn't be realised for a while yet. Things would be different in that she'd never see him. Initially, the impact would be minimal, but, after a while, the inevitable question of why he's not around anymore would crop up. Until then, Natasha would attempt to live as normal a life as possible for all concerned. Right now, it suited her having to think of Jas. It distracted her. This was a tonic she needed. She was also angry. Angry that he'd kept the full extent of his involvement to a bare minimum. Of course, she had known that, deep down, the nice money and cars weren't all down to his above-board business dealings. A bit dippy she may well have been, but naïve she certainly was not. Her maxim on such matters was, 'assume the best until you hear the worst'. She was quite happy to live in blissful ignorance if there was no negative impact. This time, however, there had been the ultimate negative impact. She also felt that, had she not closed her mind, she may have been able to see some of the signs and, consequently, been in a position to try to talk him around. This was all academic now.

She again fixed her black shawl over her shoulder to stop it from drooping. It was important for her to maintain a dignified poise. Natasha always maintained a dignified poise, regardless of whatever situation she found herself in. Dignity or a good demonstration of it was essential to her. It was, after all, who she was. She was defined by it. Although this was a very sad day, she was looking forward to seeing her brother, James, and his wife, Vanda. It meant a lot to her that they'd made the effort to make the long journey from Edinburgh. She also appreciated it as, due to an issue of trust and what James saw as a significant betrayal, he still came to pay his respects.

That can't have been an easy decision for him to make, she thought. *He trusted him and he was let down. James is obsessed with issues of trust, so he must have felt really let down. Maybe he's here for me and Jasmine. Even if that's the only reason, that's a good enough reason for me.*

* * *

The best part of a week had passed since Miles had stumbled upon his little bounty at the lockup. He wondered if he had done the right thing. Well, he knew that he had, in terms of morality. Baskin was a man who brought nothing of any positivity to the table of life, except his own one. He was wondering if he'd done the right thing in terms of the knock-on effect it may have. Not so much on himself. There was really nothing to link him to it. He was more worried about the effect that it could have on Beanmonkey and Jez. He hadn't told them where he'd gone, what he'd found or what he'd done after it all. He didn't want to worry them. It was unnecessary. There was no need, really. They'd been very good to him, and doing what he had was his way of paying them back. They'd never have to know. Yes, there was risk, but, if it did work out, the benefits for them would, indeed, be considerable. The shock of what he'd seen had subsided to a large degree. That said, something had changed in him that day. Fortunately, the change hadn't been as dramatic as he'd feared. He'd feared that he'd lost the essence of who he was and, to his relief, that hadn't happened. The shock of it all had spurred him on to make a huge decision, which may have signalled a complete departure for who he was as a person. That hadn't been the case, or so he thought. He wasn't sure if others would see it quite like that; therefore, he thought it best to keep the extent of his actions to himself. It wasn't the right time to tell them. There would be plenty of opportunities to do so when the results of his actions became clear.

Nothing's changed in me that makes me a different person. I've changed. I guess there's not much else that could've happened after what I saw, but I'm still Miles. The only thing that's changed is that I'm not a soft as shite, naive little twat. I don't know what the others will think, though. Will they thank me? Do I care if they do? Not really, I guess. If I've made their lives easier, at least I'll have contributed in some way. That's important. That's all I care about, really.

* * *

Jez's superficial wounds were well on the way to healing. They had decided that there was no great rush to get away. They could take their time. They wouldn't take too long; just enough time for Jez to make a full recovery. They had decided that they would definitely be going to Cornwall, but they no longer felt a sense of urgency to leave at the first opportunity. The list had been completed to the letter and they'd been paid in full. This meant that there would be no reason for Baskin or Frankie to be calling around. They still had a few more days before the list would be handed over. A time had been arranged for this. They would use this time to relax and they would leave at a time that suited them. Also, although they hadn't seen Baskin for a week, and in spite of the beating, Jez wasn't in a hurry to escape Baskin's influence. When walking out of the office, he had seen a certain rationale and calm in Baskin's expression. He'd never seen if before. He had been initially surprised, but, after a good night's sleep, helped in large by a few pain killers, he was able to better process Baskin's expression. He had looked guilty, too. His expression towards Frankie couldn't have been more in contrast to the one he'd received. He sensed that a lot of questions would be directed Frankie's way. He wondered what the outcome had been. Not that he cared about Frankie, but down to a sense of morbid fascination. There was also a certain degree of triumphalism in his thinking. Frankie, due in a big part to what was viewed as favouritism, lorded it over all around him. It was as if he was untouchable. Something had changed that night. He had looked scared that night; very scared. His plan had backfired in spectacular fashion. He knew it, Baskin knew it and Jez could sense it. He was very surprised at how quickly Baskin had called a halt to the beating. He had a strong feeling that he had strongly regretted the savage attack on Danny and this was coming to bear in his treatment of Jez. He couldn't help but feel that Frankie's long and intimidating reign may well be coming to an end. Yes, Baskin hated drugs, but he hated being lied to more. He'd see this as more of an affront to his character and a demonstration of a decided lack of respect. Jez realised that perhaps Baskin would be preoccupied with resolving this situation. Everyone knew how obsessive he was about unresolved issues, about loose ends.

He liked Beanmonkey's suggestion of going to St. Ives. The idea of getting away from everything they were caught up in really appealed to him. Moreover, the idea of going somewhere that couldn't be more different from London was really captivating his imagination. This surprised him.

Yes, he had wanted to escape his current life and get as far away from the clutches of Baskin as possible, but he didn't think that he'd be so keen to go away to a small fishing village. It was strange, in a way, as he'd never imagined that he'd be going somewhere like that out of choice. It wasn't the kind of place he'd ever envisaged wanted to spend time. Like Miles, his father had sometimes taken him up to the Roman wall, only he hadn't derived even close to the same pleasure or sense of wonderment Miles had. He wasn't mesmerised by the endless line of ancient wall or impressed with the crisp fresh air or what seemed like an endless open expanse of wilderness. When he had left Carlisle, London had seemed like the perfect place to go. He could disappear with ease into its busy and populated expanse. He'd enjoy the urgency and pace of it. However, now, he was quite looking forward to going to the type of place that had never before held any interest for him.

In spite of his injuries, albeit ones on the mend, he was feeling surprisingly upbeat. He could see an end to it all. In the beginning of his tenure at club Baskin, he hadn't been able to believe how lucky he was to be paid for what he did and to be paid so handsomely, to boot. He was like the proverbial greyhound sprung from the traps and darting unbounded around the track. He had become a big fish in a small pond, and meeting up with Baskin had offered him a much sought after lifeline. He had immersed himself in his new lifestyle. He had lapped it up. The money, the clubs, the parties in exclusive boutique clubs and the laid-on, high-class prostitutes. He hadn't been able to get enough of it. However, like all things, it had run its course and it was now time to call it a day.

Miles' arrival had had more of an effect on him than he had first realised. His naivety was infectious. His small-town naivety had reminded Jez of an aspect of his life that he had consigned most willingly to the annals of history.

However, the unabashed and unbridled manner in which Miles had expressed his views on that first night in the Swan had struck a chord in Jez, although he hadn't realised it at the time. However, he noticed that something in Miles had changed. It wasn't what he said. That hadn't changed. It was more about a look in his eyes. Something about his expression had changed. He couldn't put his finger on it. He couldn't help but think that something had happened to him. He had asked him if there was anything he wanted to talk about, completely out of character for Jez to ask such a thing; that was more like Beanmonkey, really.

It's weird really. He's got that kind of look that I've seen on people I've worked with before. It's the kind of look that comes when the novelty of something has worn off or you've seen something you didn't want to. I had that look once and I know why I did. Something's happened. Something's either happened to him or he's done something. Either way, there's a change in him.

The arrival of Miles and his verbose expressing of opinions, and the attacks on Danny and Jez, added to Arthur's suggestion, had all combined to act as a huge catalyst to Beanmonkey, which couldn't be ignored. That said, the time he was having reflecting on past events had made him realise that he hadn't really been happy for longer than that, possibly even for about a year. The first year had been great. He had felt like the big man, the strong man, the adventurous man, the mysterious man, and the powerful man. There was also the money. Apart from on accountancy ledgers, and that wasn't real money, anyway, he'd never seen so much money. On a good week, he could earn nearly a grand; on a bad one, generally not less than five hundred pounds. This feeling of empowerment had helped him deal with the shame of having been kicked out of his accountancy course. The person he had now become was so far removed from that of an accountant. However, he was now equally far removed from that of a car thief. For the first two years, he had never had a crisis of conscience about what he was doing. He hadn't had any feelings either way. He had been given a job to do and he had done it well. Over time, though, something inside began to seep through into his psyche. He suddenly began to question the absolutism of Baskin's dictates. He didn't, of course, voice these questions to Baskin, but they were suddenly present whereas before they were not.

Unlike Jez, he was no longer able to take such a pragmatic outlook. This way of life had been getting to him and was affecting his moods. There was a decided difference between the elation felt of being in one of his ideal images of a car to stealing them. Money wasn't an object, so now perhaps he could go and buy one of his own. In truth, he hadn't really been the same for a while. Even before the recent events... They had merely punctuated his unrest. He was happy, in a strange way, that things had unfolded as they had. Jez could sense his unease and it was beginning to impact on their friendship. He had become difficult to be around. He was changing. So, the enthusiasm Jez had shown towards his proposal had been very well received.

* * *

The funeral cortege pulled up to the tranquil surroundings of St. Mary's, Harrow on the Hill. Natasha grabbed James' hand and held it tightly. She smiled warmly. She really appreciated his coming. It was a big gesture on his part and, in her eyes, highly significant. Deciding to go into business with someone close to one is fraught with risk and difficulty. It seldom works and, if it does, there's always a possibility that it could be the undoing of this close association. In a normal and untainted work environment, the challenges are forever present. During the hours of professional association on a given day, that person is not an acquaintance, friend, father or brother; he's an associate. It's impossible to separate the colleague from the friend and vice versa. An accommodation of sorts is usually reached whereby, in social situations, the mention of work is kept to a minimum and, in the work arena, discussions of a social nature are stifled somewhat. That said, it's not always easy keeping to those rules, but it's better to have some parameters in which to operate.

It's one thing working with a friend, but an entirely different thing lending that friend money. When James decided to move to Edinburgh, he had been asked for a 'payment of goodwill'. This payment, it was made clear, would be in the form of an investment. Once this investment had helped the seed reach maturity, this payment of goodwill and its subsequent bounty would be handed back. It had never happened.

This was the betrayal. This was the ultimate betrayal to James. Promises had been made, but never fulfilled. One after the other and repeated until all semblance of trust had been eroded. He had his suspicions why these arrangements hadn't been honoured. This had reached the point where betrayal had become concern; concern not for his investment and his repayment of goodwill, but concern for his sister. There was something that just didn't add up in all this.

That wasn't too much to expect. We're family. That's really important. That's supposed to mean something. I should have tried a bit harder to reach him, though. If only for Tashie's sake. I feel a bit sad. Mainly for Tashie, but I feel a bit sad, too.

I've always had my suspicions, but I didn't think he'd end up like this. It's such a waste.

The car slowed and pulled opposite the waiting mounds of clay. The grave diggers, two of them holding shovels, stood respectfully beside them. Natasha stepped out of the car holding Jasmine's hand firmly, but not tightly. She looked back at the rest of the cortege. They were all there; his friends from the pub, work colleagues, even Frankie. She was a bit taken aback to see him on crutches, hobbling towards her.

He'd really appreciate this turn out. He'd love it, in fact. He liked Frankie. He always spoke about him. The stories he told me! He's so uncouth! What's he like?

The Bildeckers were there, too, as were the Smiths and the Langfields.

Natasha really appreciated the gesture. She knew that they were really only here for her. Still, it meant a lot. She was under no illusion as to how they were viewed among the landed set. What was important and touching was that they had shown up.

He was never that good at shooting. He said that it was obvious, but they never said anything. Although that day, that day that he hit more of those clay birds out of the sky than that lot? I'm sure they pretended to miss. Bless 'em!

* * *

Miles wished that it didn't have to take place in a cemetery. It wasn't enough to stop him, though. This was justice and he wanted to play his part in dispensing it. He'd heard, *ad nauseam*, from the older generation where they had been when Kennedy had been shot and when the Berlin wall had come down. Seeing as though he hadn't been born when either of these momentous events had taken place, he had never had any nugget of interest to bring to that particular table. This time, however, he'd be witnessing his own momentous event. Not only that, it would be something he would proudly tell his own kids. He'd gather them around and proudly recount to them the day he had played his part in putting away a very dangerous, evil man. The contents of the photographs wouldn't be mentioned, though.

He looked over towards the small group assembled on a hill. He wondered if that was the funeral. He didn't want to go too close until it had finished. He deemed that too disrespectful; an unnecessary bridge too far. It seemed pointless.

Miles had played this brilliantly. He couldn't have played it better, in fact. He felt that what he'd seen had possibly pushed him over the edge, sending him into an area of psychosis; a dark place, a place where he'd never been before, a place where he didn't think he'd ever visit, ever have to visit. He had reached the point where the only conclusion he could draw was to remove Baskin completely. He had sat for hours in Barnham Park, staring at the gun, thinking of the best possible way to do this. He'd look at the photographs from time to time, becoming increasingly more sickened, then, suddenly, it had come to him.

He'd remembered the rumour of Ben Stillcome's demise. As the story goes, Ben used to work for Baskin. He had been good; one of the best. One day, he had arrived at the lockup with his latest acquisition, and that was the last anyone had heard of him – alive. Rumour had it that Baskin had been late in paying him from a previous job and a resulting argument had then ensued. It was this argument that had sealed his fate. Rumour also had it that, during this argument, he had pulled a gun on Baskin, there had been a struggle, the gun had then fallen into Baskin's possession, and Baskin had shot him; shot him with his own gun. His body had then been dumped in some woodland area and found a few days later. The police had nothing to go on, as there was nothing to link anyone to his murder. There were no fingerprints, as Baskin always wore gloves. They weren't worn for any reason of crime evasion, but as part of his uniform. They went quite nicely with his crombie and tanned brogues.

So, nervously, but with purpose, he had walked into Wembley Park Police Station and handed the gun in. He had held onto the photographs. Before revealing that he was in possession of the gun, he had requested an interview based on him having some information that might come in handy. There was a proviso, however; no identities that he didn't feel were relevant to this had to be divulged. This was agreed to. Also, the informant, if he so chose, could remain anonymous. This they also agreed to. He did agree, however, say that, in the event of additional evidence being required, and only if it was completely necessary, then he would waive this anonymity. The interview was surprisingly short, as all they were interested in was where he'd found the gun and who he thought it may belong to. The gun was then put into one of those evidence bags and sent off to forensics, and that was that.

Before he left the station, he had asked, as gesture of goodwill, that they simply keep him up to date.

He was having an attack of conscience. In fact, he'd had it all day since receiving the call from what sounded like a young, probably just out of Hendon, policeman. Although he had asked that he simply be kept up to speed with what was happening, he didn't think that extended to being told that the results from forensics had come back and they were going up to formerly arrest him. Actually, he expected that, but he didn't expect to be told where this would be taking place. All he had expected was simply 'yes, we've got him' or 'we will need you to give evidence, after all'. His thinking here was that the young PC had probably passed on more information than he had been asked to.

It's bad enough that the whole thing is taking place at a cemetery. It's unfortunate, really, but what can I do? All I can do is maintain a respectful distance until I see the cops arrive. I'm sure they wouldn't go up in the middle of a funeral. They wouldn't, would they?

Being the pedantic and proactive person he was, he had checked the births, deaths and marriages section in the local rag to see if he could find any clues to who the funeral was for. Eventually, he had come to 'Philip David King, 34, who sadly passed away on January 27, 2009. He will be sadly missed by his brother, James King, sister, Natasha Baskin, God-niece, Jasmine Baskin, and brother-in-law, James Fulton Noel Baskin'.

The rest of the add went into when and where the funeral was taking place, and he already knew that.

The young vicar opened a yellow, bound, dog eared notebook.

"Finally, Natasha requested that I read some words, which were personal to her. These lovely words, which I'm honoured to have been asked to read, were penned by Philip himself."

He read, "I can make it if I hope. I'll keep dreaming for the sky. Will I get there, I don't know? Nothing stays the same. And, in the twilight, when it falls, I will reach back to my dreams, then I'll reach towards the sky again and dream.

"I shall take my chances; count my blessings of family, health and love. To love the winter's reddish sky in all its brazen glory is to feel alive. To feel imbedded in nature's hidden glories."

Jimmy grasped Natasha's hand tightly.

"He would have loved this, Natasha; his own beautiful words; his own beautiful words being recounted at his own funeral. That's something we dream of, if you've got the words. Beautiful touch, love."

Baskin's words meant little to Natasha. Philip was dead. She'd lost her brother. She no longer felt any anger, only a deep sadness. It had been a huge shock when she had heard the news. She couldn't believe that she'd lost him, and at such a young age and in the way she had. Although she had known that his life had become embroiled in some form of trouble and turmoil, she'd had no idea that he'd been involved with drugs; so involved to the extent that the police had told her they thought that's why he may have been shot. They hadn't arrested anyone yet.

When Philip had come to visit, he'd always had a friendly look. It was a look of kindness, a forlorn look. A look that asked many questions, yet provided no answers. He sensed that he'd fallen from grace, to a certain extent, in her eyes. He was wrong. She was disappointed that he hadn't paid, or even attempted to pay, James back the money. However, she was much more concerned about what his reason for not doing so may have been. She had her suspicions, though she never once questioned him and not once did she mention it. He had never brought it up. They both knew that it was out there in the public domain. That had seemed enough at the time.

She loved him. It was as simple as that. One by one, he'd lost his friends. She had thought that strange at the time, but, in hindsight, it was obvious why. She wondered also that, despite the financial investment from James, he had ended up losing his business. She loved him and she had tried to involve him in most things they did. He wasn't at all interested in currying favour with the high fliers of the landed set, but his sister was and he appreciated being invited along. He also loved seeing little Jasmine. This was the only time that his forlorn look was banished and replaced with one of vibrancy and joy. He even liked Baskin. He knew that all was not what it seemed with him, but he didn't care. Baskin was good to his sister. He was great to his sister. He gave her everything she wanted and she loved him in return. That was good enough for him.

She looked up at Jimmy Baskin and forced a smile of sorts. She owed him that much. He had been so supportive through all this. She knew that recovery or, more realistically, containment of this grief wouldn't be secured over night and that he'd be there for her resolutely. Therefore, she felt that trying to smile at him today was the least he deserved.

* * *

In respectful silence for where they were and for the day that it was, the police pulled up slowly to the cemetery gates. There were four cars in total. Two of them marked and two unmarked. In light of whom they were coming to arrest and the potential pitfalls involved, it was better to be over prepared.

* * *

Miles, although still keeping a respectful distance from the mourners, was observing the arrival of the troops from the unseen vantage point of a hedge a short distance from the gates. He could feel his excitement levels begin to soar as he noticed DCI Brennan. This was the man who had interviewed him. He was a big man with an imposing presence. He could imagine him being first choice in interviewing suspected villains. Fortunately for Miles, he had had really important information, which they needed and that he had been only too willing to share.

He kept his position as the police assembled close to the gates. He wondered if any of them were carrying guns.

They'd have to be, really, when you think of it. I mean, they're not exactly dealing with Girl Guides!

Seeing the police arrive had banished any feelings of unease he had felt about this taking place at a funeral. The funeral was drawing to a close, and he and the police had kept a respectful distance.

I don't care what day it is now. This has to come to an end. It's gone on long enough. Maybe I feel a bit sorry for Natasha, but she's benefited from his lifestyle choice. I mean, why didn't she leave him? She must know what he does, apart, of course, from raping men. The bottom line is, his time's up and he's just getting what's coming to him. This couldn't happen to nicer bloke!

He looked up at the now-mobile sea of black suits. The service had finished and they were making their way towards the exit and, in turn, towards the waiting police.

Ha ha! Quality! He's no idea what's waiting for him. He soon will, though. These people. Who do they think they are? What gives them the right to just fucking attack whoever they want? Nothing. The bastards; they don't have the right, but it's his turn to be on the receiving end of things now.

* * *

As the procession continued along the over the stones and nearer the exit, it was oblivious to the waiting reception party. Most of the procession's heads were bowed in a sombre mood. Some stopped and offered the obligatory condolences to Natasha.

"Right, gents," said Brennan. "Davies, Szul, come with me. The rest, stay here."

The group, still moved by the oratory from the vicar, hadn't really noticed the police presence.

Natasha had her arm arched into Baskin's as her head rested on his shoulder. She was feeling a bit more relaxed now. The emotion for that moment was less raw. She knew that she had to make the most of such moments.

Baskin suddenly looked up. He recognised Brennan. He knew Brennan. Brennan was well known among people of a certain persuasion. He seemed to always be in the 'post' speaking about such topics as 'the need for community resolve' and other ones such as 'the need to be proactive for community cohesion'. Baskin hated such articles; not because he saw these as a call to moralistic arms, but simply because he saw them as cheesy, sentimentalist, egotistical nonsense. These articles never meant a great deal to the local population and, consequently, were, on the whole, ineffectual. He wondered why he was there, especially considering a funeral had just taken place.

What are these rozzers doing here? It's bang out. Especially on a day like this. Especially on the days that a funeral takes place. What gives 'em the right? Oh, shit. Why are they really here?

Brennan, flanked by Sergeants Davies and Szul, politely nudged his way through the sea of black and on to Baskin. Baskin looked startled.

Why are they really here? I've done nothing wrong, really. What are they going to do?

He couldn't work out how or for what reason, but he felt that a significant aspect of his life was drawing to a close. It wasn't the first time he had been hauled before Brennan for questioning for crimes he had actually committed, but that couldn't be proved. However, there was something different happening today.

The decision to arrest someone in a cemetery is not one that they would take lightly. They must have something. I won't cause a scene, for Tashie's sake.

I don't feel too bad for myself. Why does it have to happen today of all days?

Brennan, with officers Davies and Szul, walked up to Baskin. "Mr. James Fulton Noel Baskin."

Baskin smiled. "Yes, you know it is. Just get on with what you have to do, Brennan." He turned to a visibly shocked Natasha. "I don't know what this is all about, Tashie, but I won't be gone for long."

He then turned around to face the rest of the group, which was in an orderly, almost linear, formation.

"People. Please don't worry about this. This is obviously some mistake. All I can do is apologise on their behalf for this crass and wholly insensitive intrusion. My beautiful wife, Natasha, I know, will do me proud and shower upon you the hospitality you deserve. I'll be back before music."

'Music' was Natasha's tribute to her brother where, after the obligatory assortment of biscuits and crustless quartered sandwiches, a selection of his favourite music would be played.

"Okay, then, Brennan," said Baskin. "Read the bit about the right to remain silent, etcetera."

Before he could do this, Miles, who had been keeping a watchful distance, walked over to the group and straight up to Natasha. He had tears in his eyes.

"I'm sorry to do this to you of all days, but I think you've got the right to know. Please take this."

He handed her an A5 brown envelope. She reached out and took it.

"Don't open it now. Wait until you're by yourself. This will show you just exactly who you're married to. What you're married to. I know this is a very bad time to have to do this and I do apologise, but I think you deserve to know."

A very worried-looking Baskin suddenly lunged at her in attempt to grab the envelope from her. "Don't listen to him, love. It's only stuff to frame me. It's nothing. Give them to me. You don't need to see 'em. It don't mean anything. I am who you think I am. I am the one you love, the one who buys you nice things and the one who pays for you to play golf. I give you everything. Please, love, these mean nothing. Please don't."

Szul and Dawson restrained him.

Brennan stepped forward. He looked over at Miles and nodded approvingly. "Where was I? Oh yes, Mr. James Fulton Noel Baskin, you have been charged with the murder of Benjamin Paul Stillcombe; you have the right to remain silent. You do not have to say anything when questioned…"

Before he could finish, Baskin broke down sobbing. He knew exactly what was in the envelope. It had the same yellow stain, a stain that had been made when he had clumsily dropped a freshly cut piece of lemon onto it. He had narrowly missed his glass of G&T, which he'd prepared after viewing his collection of memories.

He could just about handle doing time, but he couldn't handle losing Natasha. At least if he was inside and he knew that he still had the love of the most significant person he'd ever known, he could handle it. He could do his time, in spite of where he was, with relative ease. However, now he knew he'd lost her. He looked over at her. She looked vacant and lifeless as if what lived beneath her shell had died. She made her way towards the exit. She looked back at Baskin and smiled. She owed him at least that much. She turned back and continued toward the gates.

Miles looked on as she settled into the back of the leading black Limousine. His heart felt heavy. He knew that, in the greater scheme of things, he'd done the best thing for all concerned. However, he nonetheless knew that, for now, he had compounded her grief. However, he also knew that he'd saved her from much worse future potential grief. Overall, he felt that he'd done the right thing. He looked around at the now-empty cemetery. Above him, a thin film of darkness floated in patient expectation. Szul pushed Baskin's head down to facilitate smooth entry into the back of one of the unmarked police cars. He knew he'd have to move fast. He didn't know if Baskin's loyalists – and he was sure that there must have some present – might be planning something. He fixed his holdall over his shoulder and walked through the exit. He knew he was safe now. At least, that's how he felt.

He walked through the assembled cars and on towards the high street.

It's all good. I've done it now. It's over. It all stops today.

It's over and I'm glad I played my part. Fuck it, I'm proud I played my part. He's nothing now. Finished. He messed with my mind and now he's paid the price. He'd no respect for anyone. He's the loser now.

* * *

Jez and Beanmonkey sat in silence in 'the grapes' near Paddington Station. Three full glasses of 'Monkies' sat expectantly on their table. In turn, they looked up in an attempt to say something, if only to offer some words to each other, any words, words that could say something to sum up how they were feeling.

To sum up how enormously proud they were of their naive little friend; that soft wee shite; that soft wee shite who had walked into the Swan three weeks ago and whose naive wisdom had cut into their conscience; *their* soft wee shite. They couldn't find any. There were none.

10

Sudbury Town

Sudbury High Street was waking to the sound of early morning traffic and the clattering of shutters being lifted by more hopeful than expectant shop owners. Two sixty pence boys – so called because, when pitching for money, they'd always be 'sixty pence short for my train ticket'; the truth was, it was going towards their special brew and white cider fund – were making their way towards the tube station. It had been a busy weekend and street cleaners set about the tedious task of collecting the many and varied fast food wrappings and other assorted consumables that had been selfishly discarded by those lacking even a basic sense of civic responsibility. Two bus drivers passed the usual pleasantries regarding the weekend football upsets and the state of the economy whilst waiting for their carriages to populate.

Baskin had just awoken after his first night in the police cells. He didn't know how long they'd keep him in or if he'd get bail. He thought it was unlikely considering what he'd been arrested for. He couldn't get the face of that skinny teen who had handed the photographs over to Natasha out of his mind. It was an image that refused to go away. He was certain of one thing, though; he had no idea who that person was. He had no idea why this person would even know about or would want to break into what appeared to be a derelict warehouse.

It's gotta be someone I know, but who? I know I've made a lot of enemies over the years, but who'd have the balls to do this? Who'd be stupid enough to do this? It's mental. He's obviously been paid by someone, but who? And if he hasn't been, then why would he do this to me? I've done nothing to him. I don't even know 'em.

Suddenly, after years of living in moralistic oblivion, he now found himself in a reality where situations and circumstances were now dictating themselves to him in succinct clarity. Not only was he physically restricted, but he was now mentally curtailed. The whole little world that he'd, with relative ease and precision, crafted for himself was gone. Had it still existed, even somewhat off the radar, his ability to navigate back to it was lacking. There was nowhere to go to now. This new place was cold, harsh and unforgiving. He'd never be happy in it. It was pointless even trying.

* * *

In his upstairs bedroom in the Swan, Ian turned over and looked lovingly at Dave as he moved from side to side in an attempt to fall back into the tranquil place he'd been before being rudely awoken by Ian. Ian smiled again and decided that it would be cruel to hinder him in this noblest of quests. This playfulness was merely a break from the troubles on his mind. He was worried. He couldn't stop thinking about whether or not Miles would be able to drag himself out of the horrible place he was in. When he'd seen the desperation in him, he'd remembered where he'd last seen it. He had been eighteen looking in the mirror and attempting to come out to himself. He didn't think that that had been Miles' dilemma. Ian's 'gaydar' was never offline.

However, he could see the despair and fear in Miles' eyes. He hoped that his words offered and the comfort shown by him had helped forge even the most basic beginnings of a furrow that could lead Miles away from that dire place he was in. He wondered if he'd ever see him again. He had this strange feeling that perhaps he'd seen the last of him. He hoped not.

Kelvin, one of the five fulltime gardeners at Barham Park, was tending to the rose garden. He was smiling, but, inside, he was laughing hysterically. The memory of that 'crazy middle-aged fat boy white man' dancing around his garden last week had now decided to pop back into his head. It wasn't the first time he'd seen this. In fact, he'd seen this 'mad boy' perform on five occasions. He'd noticed that it was usually a gap of between two to three weeks. He loved it. It was the highlight of his day. Each day, he'd set off for work with a heightened sense of hope that he'd see him perform. Initially, upon viewing his maiden performance, he thought that perhaps he'd absconded from a facility for the mentally ill, but, upon careful consideration, he thought that he was far too well dressed and groomed for that to be the case.

Although he thoroughly enjoyed each performance, he did have his favourite ones. Whether it was because it was completely unexpected and new or simply because it was a most superb performance, or perhaps both, nothing, apart from maybe the third time, had come close to the first performance. To him, it had everything. The choreography was spot on, the facial expressions were beguiling and the effort shown was inspiring. It had all the ingredients that made it a superb performance. He wasn't, however, overly impressed with last week's performance. It had looked as if he had just been going through the motions. He didn't look as if he was enjoying himself, which added to the overall feeling of disappointment. Kelvin hoped that he'd see a marked improvement the next time he performed in two or three week's time.

* * *

Frankie hobbled over to Baskin's desk and sat. Baskin was gone now. He was out of the picture. He was no more. No more the imposing, frightening and altogether malignant force. He pulled open the drawer where Baskin's pictures and his gun or, rather, Ben Stillcombe's gun, had been kept. He smiled. This was all his now. He was considering whether or not he would sell on the car business; he had already received enquiries from two firms, both based in the east end. Both had been very competitive and tempting offers. His interest in this area had been at best tacit and at worst disapproving. He was looking forward to reprising the debt collecting side of things. He would do this with renewed energy. He would be uncompromising and single minded in his pursuit of its success. There was enough money left in the safe to enable him to get it back off the ground. All the old contacts were still there; all written down on eight A4 pieces of paper. He would add to this list with renewed vigour. Being the boss now would allow him to take a more hands-off role, if that was his want, but he wouldn't. After all, being on the front line was what he wanted. He excelled at it. He had decided that last time out was a blip. It was a minor setback. He'd simply just hop back on the proverbial saddle. The first person he would be visiting would be Glen Johnston to wipe the slate clean. He didn't owe him money, but Frankie owed him. He'd enjoy paying him back, though he'd wait until his legs healed and he'd bring someone along just for backup, in case there were more junkies hiding with loaded syringes. He, like Baskin, hated junkies. He didn't trust them. They were unpredictable.

Baskin, or rather, Tel and Austin, had given him a good kicking, although he felt fortunate in that it could have, in truth, been a lot worse. For some reason, Baskin had had a change of heart, or perhaps a pang of conscience, and ordered them to stop. Frankie had been spared a potentially worse fate and he was relived. He knew that, even more than junkies, Baskin hated liars. Frankie had been very fortunate, indeed, and he knew it. However, it didn't stop him being angry with himself for not thinking his plan through in more detail. He'd been casual and lazy in his approach. Highly educated he may not have been, but Baskin was clever and highly intuitive. He could spot a lie with relative ease. You never lied to him. It was understood, a given. It was virtually a declaration of suicide to even consider doing so. Frankie had been foolhardy and he knew this.

Although fortunate and feeling a great sense of personal achievement at now being at the helm, he was having mixed feelings. Baskin had taken him on when other firms wouldn't touch him. He must have seen some potential in him. He had lost contact with his parents when he was four as, due to neglect, he'd been taken off to Banardos. It was there that he had honed the skills that would eventually take him on to bigger and better things. Banardos was a tough and unforgiving place. It was cruel and hostile. Yes, the charge of care was dispensed in that they always had enough food, shelter and basic elementary education, but that was it. There was no love to fill the void caused by the loss of his parents. Once the children were left to their own devices, it was an open playing field, a battle field of sorts. Frankie, being one of the bigger children, had honed his combatant skills by picking on the smaller ones, which, in truth, was practically everyone else, apart from Henry Atkins, who was slightly taller and a couple of years older. They both gave each other a respectful wide berth. Baskin was really the closest to family he had ever had, so he'd do the decent thing and visit him in prison. Overall, though, he was happy to find himself in the position he now was. He was at the helm, where he'd always wanted to be.

He couldn't get the image of that *skanky little scroat* out of his mind. Reluctantly, he acknowledged, to himself, at least, that he had witnessed the ultimate in bravery, or perhaps madness; he hadn't quite made up his mind which. Courtesy of Baskin, he poured himself a large G&T and sat fully back in the recliner.

The way he just walked up and handed that envelope over to Natasha and in front of everyone. That must've taken balls to do. It's hard to admit this, but that's braver than anything I've ever done. It's easy for me to just go up to people and give 'em a kicking. It's easy. I'm a big cunt, but I could never do anything like that. Fair play. Seriously, but who is he and why'd he do that? Whatever the reason was, I'd like to buy him a big drink

* * *

Suze Wilfasson laid the tray down by the side of Danny's bed. He was home now and making good progress. They had heard the news of Baskin's fate. Jez had told them. She couldn't believe it. The big man of West London had been culled, and by that 'lovely wee lad'.

I knew there was something about that wee lad. I can't describe it, really. I can't quite put my finger on it. He had a look of honesty about him. There was something different, something not quite of this world, but of a more innocent time.

Maybe it's his youth, but that's not the full picture. No, there's something more. Anyway, whatever and for whatever reason, that evil bastard's gone. That man who just saw people as part of a game, his game. I hope he rots.

* * *

Arthur Seagrove turned the final page of the ironically entitled novel, *The Death of a Funeral Parlour*. Ironic in that he'd joked to Beanmonkey that he 'wasn't very far from the funeral parlour'. It used to upset him every time Arthur mentioned it. He knew what Arthur was saying was an accurate statement, but he hated hearing it all the same. Arthur didn't say it for effect, but for humour. He'd no idea that Beanmonkey didn't view it with the same hilarity until one day when he saw a glazed sadness in his eyes. He never mentioned it again until Beanmonkey, when visiting the Marie Currie shop on Wembley High Street, whilst looking in the book section, spotted it; *The Death of a Funeral Parlour*; he had had no choice but to buy it.

He closed the book and moved around to pick up the cigar Beanmonkey had bought him. Smoking wasn't allowed in St. Jerome's and he hadn't smoked in over twenty years. He flicked up the Zippo, another gift from his young confidant. As a solider, he had been predisposed to abide by the rules. Today, however, it wasn't just justified to flout them; it seemed rude not to. He relaxed into his bed and smiled. He felt proud. Being of a modest disposition, he, as a rule, never allowed himself to indulge in a sense of pride. He had seen comrades fall and not get up again. He told himself that he'd never entertain any ostentatious whims. This time, however, not only did it feel justified, it felt necessary. It was important to recognise what had been one of the finest gifts he had ever bestowed upon anyone and therefore give it the appropriate recognition. He was proud, because he'd given Beanmonkey a chance to escape to a place that he knew he deserved to be.

My work here, as they say, is done! I hope he enjoys his time in victory cottage. I hope he takes advantage of its tranquillity and that he realises what he has. I feel so humbled right now. So humbled that I'm in position to help such a great lad, a lad who I feel privileged to be able to have helped, considering how much he helped me.

God bless him. Right then. Off back to plough my lonely furrow once again.

He threw his half-finished cigar out the window. He hoped he'd see Anton again. He hoped that there would be enough juice still left in the old tank.

* * *

Natasha has seen the pictures, in private, as Miles had advised. She couldn't believe what she'd seen; these gross images with those poor men. She knew that what was happening in these photos wasn't consensual. This had forced her to reflect upon herself and how she viewed her relationship. Upon reflection, she had always had her suspicions as to how their salubrious lifestyle was being funded. He was a soulless, nasty and uncompromising gangland thug. Whenever he had come up with an excuse as to why she couldn't visit the business premises, it had suited her. It suited her perfectly. It was convenient all too convenient. However, to be capable of murder was one thing, but rape, this was another thing entirely. Distasteful as murder was, she viewed rape with even more distain. It wasn't the issue of sexuality that sickened her. It was the image of terror in their eyes. This had burnt a dark, disturbing image into her mind. Moreover, the fact that, after carrying out these brutalities, he was coming back and making love to her as passionately and as perfectly as he did. She felt violated.

He was my world. He helped make me who I am. But I'm not that person anymore. It was all boastful nonsense. Horse riding? Clay pigeon shooting. Dinner parties with folks who look down their noses at us? What was the point?

What is the point? It's all lies and it was completely pointless.

She wasn't sure how to view her young messenger. On one hand, he had destroyed her charmed life. On the other, he'd stripped away the lies. She had been perfectly content to live in ignorant bliss. It suited her. The old adage of 'what you don't know doesn't hurt' suited her. She had been perfectly content to live within this tenet.

However, she was awake now. Her eyes had been opened for better or for worse. She had realised that perhaps she didn't need someone else to forge her identity. She wondered who this young, angelic-looking messenger was. She wondered how he had come to have these photographs and why he picked that day of all days to deliver his package.

He had tears in his eyes, so he must have found it difficult to do. I just wish he'd picked a better day. A bit bang out, but maybe that was the only chance he had. If that is the case, I'm fine with that. Apart from the tears, there was something missing in his face, as if he was lost, but trying to find his way home in some way. It's still a strange and brave thing to do. Who knows, maybe one day in the future my life will be better than I ever imagined it could be. I'll have to hang on to that.

She picked up Jasmine and secured her into the car baby seat. Her life had been changed. It had been changed immeasurably. It had changed beyond all recognition. Nothing would ever be the same again. Her illusion had been shattered. It had been blown to pieces, destroyed, sullied and contaminated beyond all belief. The life presented to her had been built on falsities. It had all been an illusion built upon false expectations and carried off with a misguided realisation. Her image of perfection was no more. She'd loved Jimmy for who he was or, rather, who she thought he was. She still loved him. After all, love isn't an emotion that can be turned off at will. How perfect would it be if that was possible. However, that's not the way it works. Life's complicated. It's rich in contradictions and unforgiving in its relentless pursuit of pain. It will drag one to the depths of despair. On the flipside, it can be the herald of good tidings and it can be the consummate leveller. Natasha wasn't in the correct frame of mind to take such a worldly stance in all this. She had taken a pragmatic approach to her misfortune. The pictures she had seen had disturbed her greatly. She had acted quickly and was operating on auto pilot. Their joint bank account had been emptied and she wasn't going to look back. It was all in the past now. She pushed the button and waited for the large steel gates to recline, then drove off. She didn't look back.

* * *

The Swan, with its strong, imposing pillars and its plethora of varied characters, wouldn't change that much. It was still a vibrant little local. People would still be playing pool. Romances and one night stands would still be sealed through a look across a crowded area, or through scintillating conversation. Business deals would still be clinched. New friendships would continue be struck up and existing ones maintained. Small fortunes would continue to be won and lost on the fruit machine. Families would struggle to get to the next week as a result of over-excessive spending. Fights would still break out and relationships would still break up. People would still break out in tears for no apparent reason and many more would break out in song for plenty of reasons. All in all, this vibrant place and the focal point of the community would remain the same.

11

Mr. Miles Goodwin

Miles walked up the steps towards the main entrance to Euston Station. It was strange for him to think that it had been only three weeks since arriving at this very place. It seemed like a lifetime ago. A lot had changed. The change in him was quite marked. The essence of who he was in terms of morality and humility hadn't changed. The very core of him remained the same and he was relived that he hadn't lost that in some type of trade off. However, what had changed was superficial and, in all honesty, that's all he had wanted to change. Whilst retaining the same moral compass, he had lost the soft edge when dealing with situations. He felt able and confident to take on most situations now. His timidity was no more. He had even subconsciously developed a different tone to his voice to mirror that of his newfound strength and confidence. It was slightly deeper and more commanding. The squeaky voice was gone. He even walked differently, confidently and with purpose. He had even developed a swagger. He no longer skulked and dragged his feet.

He had arrived in London in a state and was now leaving in style. In what Beanmonkey considered a fitting farewell, he had paid for a room for all three in the Paddington Grand. He thought it pointless to stay in a cheap bed and breakfast when what was called for was a

huge and beautifully over the top send off. Anything less
would have been wholly inappropriate, he thought. Not
only were they massively proud of Miles, they also knew
that he had been the main player in their liberation from
Baskin and they felt that they owed him. Miles hadn't
needed to put his hand in his pocket once, and he'd woken
up in luxury, albeit with a ridiculously verbose hangover.
The hangover seemed worth it, though. It was a small price
to pay for what may well turn out to be a final farewell.
There was no way of telling, really.

Jez and Beanmonkey, after St. Ives, would be going off
to Bangkok to try to realise their dream of opening and
running their own bar. They'd told Miles they were going
to name it after him. He'd believe that when he saw it!
They'd even asked him to come along and join them, or at
least even come to St. Ives with them. He respectively
declined, as he realised that he had his own path to tread.
They were disappointed, but they understood. They'd just
miss him; that was all. He even saw tears in both sets of
eyes as they said their farewells. They did, however, stop
short of actually crying. That really would have been
pushing it. Ironically, Miles was the one who showed the
least emotion. That wasn't to say that he wasn't feeling
emotional at the parting. He was desperately sad, and a
horrible empty feeling lay in his stomach. However, it was
important for him to keep his emotions in check. He wanted
to punctuate the beginning of the next chapter of life in the
manner in which he meant to proceed, upbeat and
confident.

He continued on past the bra shop and onto Platform 3
to await the 3:30 back to Carlisle. He wondered how Jez
and Beanmonkey would find it out in Bangkok if they ever
did decide to go there. He felt envious, but not to the point
of jealously. He was happy for them, really happy for them.
In his short time with them, he'd learnt a lot. They had

taught him a lot. He'd seen a different world. After all, this is where he'd earned his spurs. It was where the boy had become a man. This was where he'd come of age. There were certainly no tears for his lost innocence anymore. He'd wanted so desperately to lose this innocence, which he saw as a constraint to who he always knew he was, though he had never imagined that he'd lose it in such an unexpected, totally unforeseen manner.

The more he thought about it, the more the pendulum was swinging in favour of him deciding that, in handing Natasha Baskin the photographs, he'd done the right thing. He always knew he had, as he'd thought long and hard before doing so. However, in so doing, he'd also changed her world forever, and that included her lifestyle and changed her whole demographic, and he'd done it on the day she was burying her brother. This was the crux, really. He could have posted them to her or simply handed them over to the police. Both would have yielded positive results, but the point for Miles was that he had wanted to maximise the impact. It was important for him that she witnessed Baskin's reaction to it all; this, he had achieved. The fact that he had sobbed in front of everyone meant that, even if by some freak accident he avoided incarceration, his whole reputation lay in tatters.

He also felt that he was doing her a huge service and that she'd want to thank him one day; at least, that's what he hoped. He didn't know her. Apart from being married to Baskin, that's all he knew about her; so, for all he knew, she could be a good person, even a great person, so she deserved a chance of happiness, of real happiness. He didn't know her, but he had sensed something good in her when looking directly into her eyes. Miles didn't usually look people directly in the eye, but he had begun to do so gradually over the past three weeks. It was all about his confidence levels. He'd looked her in the eye and he'd seen

something good. Therefore, if she was good, she deserved
to live within goodness instead of becoming gradually more
infected by Baskin's influence.

The truth was that this had all started to happen. Not in
an obvious way, but in a collection of certain things. The
social climbing, albeit subtle, was a sign of this. There was
nothing inherently wrong with that, per say, but it was done
with an abandonment of grace. The main thing, though, was
her tacit approval of her husband's actions, within the rules
of his world. In her mitigation, she didn't know what he
did, but it suited her to believe that he was an importer of
fine art and antiquities. It fitted into her vision of who they
were. As long as she got to go horse riding, buy nice
clothing and jewellery, and drive her Boxter, she was
happy. Her reaction and her subsequent decision to leave
underlined that, in spite of an addiction to wealth and
status, there was a price that she wasn't willing to pay.
She'd left not just for issues of rape, but, moreover, because
of what the rape represented; it was a symptom of who
Baskin was as a person. Therefore, being charged with
murder in light of this now seemed plausible to her. It
seemed to add up, and this had all been brought crashing
home to her by Miles' uncompromising and brave actions.
She would thank him one day, probably.

* * *

Miles was surprised that 'this young lad from Carlisle'
could have had such a profound affect on such an iconic
character as Baskin. He was a hard man, a man whose very
name had struck fear into those around him. A man who,
for years, had terrorised all and sundry. A distasteful man.
A violent man. A man who raped at will and with impunity.
A sociopath. A man who brought nothing whatsoever to the
fruitful table of humanity. The world really was better off

without him. He hadn't killed him, but he had broken him. Even in the unlikely event of avoiding a long prison sentence, there was no way he would be able to bounce back from Miles' clever, fearless and unselfish actions. In a way, he had killed him. Baskin had been defined by what he did and Miles had taken that away from him. He had held Baskin's whole character up, put it under a microscope and exposed it. It was unable to stand up to the scrutiny. In so doing, he had destroyed his whole *raison d'être*, his whole agenda. There was no need for any guilt at all. On the contrary, he felt that he had carried out a much-needed and long-overdue service. To him, it was inconceivable that such behaviour would remain unchallenged and could continue to be tolerated. People had a right to live as they so chose. It was a simple equation. If someone was preventing others from living as they chose, then the cause would have to be removed. To him, it was that black and white. Yes, he had lost his innocence, but he'd found it again, only, this time, in a more realistic and tangible form. It was no longer debilitating; it was in the form of clarity and acceptance. He now had the balance whereby he could see the purity and innocence of people and situations, but the strength of character to effect change when called upon to do so. Mission accomplished, he would be leaving London a much more rounded, well-balanced and altogether happier person.

He wondered when he'd see Jez and Beanmonkey next. Now that the origin and name of 'Beanmonkey' had been explained to him, he really couldn't think of any other name that could be more appropriate. He liked Beanmonkey. He loved him. He was now part of him. They were linked in some way. He couldn't have become who he now was, had their paths not crossed. Friendship is one of the most beautiful states of being there is. Unlike siblings, these people are set apart from others who seek out their friendship. It's ethereal, yet basic and grounding. Miles and Beanmonkey's lives were now embedded in each other's beings. They were linked. He knew him only as Beanmonkey. The name fitted perfectly. This was, of course, a two-way thing.

It was reciprocated. Miles' arrival in Sudbury town had had an effect on Beanmonkey's life. He had facilitated the change of direction Beanmonkey had craved. He had paved the way for him to become the person who he knew he was. He no longer had to be a pariah. No longer would he have to live on the fringes of society. No longer would he have to deprive hard-working people, decent people, people who, on the whole, struggled through life's assault, of their prized possessions. He no longer had to associate with people he despised and whose lack of humility he wholeheartedly rejected. Psychopaths, sociopaths, mean-spirited people, people who deprived others of the joy of live. Pimps, crime bosses, heavies, extortionists and rapists, all those to whom common decency and fraternity were bywords for weakness.

No. This was now a thing of the past for him. He now had a clear, untainted and uncontaminated canvas upon which to paint his own picture, a picture of his own choosing. So, what of Jez? Well, if Beanmonkey was an able seaman on Miles' voyage of discovery, then Jez was his captain. Miles had idolised Jez. He'd seen Jez as a mentor. He'd seen him as the older streetwise brother he'd never had. The brother he longed for. Beanmonkey had been an important player in Miles' largely self-penned drama, but Jez had played the leading supporting role. However, what effect had Miles' arrival had upon him? Quite a marked one, in fact. Although it would most likely turn out to be temporary, as the effects over time would dissipate somewhat, as pragmatism would most likely reign supreme in the end.

That said, Miles, albeit naïvely delivered, observations and general demeanour had installed in him a moral compass. It had forced him to look beyond just simply making a decision without considering the possible consequences. Unlike Beanmonkey, however, there had been no gaping holes. He knew who he was and had done so ever since embarking upon his self-contained foray into the theatre of life's struggle. He was simple. He was uncomplicated. He had no longing for, or pretensions to uncover the real him. There was nothing to uncover. He was transparent. He wasn't mean-spirited, but, at the same time, he had been unperturbed by how he earned his living. If he didn't do it, someone else would. That was his maxim. Obviously there were limitations, certain actions that he'd consider to be beyond the pale.

Unlike Beanmonkey, he generally slept well at night. That's not to say that he hadn't held any opinions on Baskin. He had. He just got on with it. He took the money, smiled and moved on. Going to Bangkok was no different to him than getting behind the wheel of an illegally acquired car. Miles' legacy, however, would give him boundaries and a set of rules in which to operate. Leaving the car thieving business behind again was a pragmatic decision. His and Danny Hall's beating had shown him that he no longer wished to continue along this path. It was too dangerous; they were both pragmatic decisions. He suited himself, but he wasn't selfish. He was free. He was undaunted and unbridled. He was a man of substance. His conscience wasn't dumbed down and he wasn't impervious to morality. However, he was savvy and he was single minded. He was headstrong and he was fiercely independent. Jez would continue being Jez. He would continue to strive for life liberty and the pursuit of hedonism.

Miles surveyed all around him. Although still only the afternoon, the station was awash with people. Different people, diverse people, people all going about their business with a strong sense of urgency. He'd miss London, but he was happy to be going back to Carlisle a changed person. It felt good to be going back stronger and more complete. There were no skeletons or unforeseen destructive surprises lying in wait this time. He had, indeed, rode into battle upon his wholly undernourished steed and laid waste to every windmill in sight. He'd have to remain vigilant, of course. He couldn't live on past successes and would need to go back and check to see if any demons would resurface. He had come this far and a defeat through complacency on his part could not be a consideration. He was proud. He was valiant and, as he stood on Platform Number 3, he reigned supreme.

He was looking forward to seeing his mother. He'd missed her and had felt somewhat guilty at his sudden departure. That said, he wouldn't have changed any detail of the journey that this sudden departure had spawned. He'd do it all again, including the wok, especially the wok, if only for comedic value. It was so deadpan, very Tom and Jerry. He smiled as he remembered that incident. It had been all hurried and rather bizarre. This time, meeting Craig, he'd confront him with his issues and with any grievance he had. Only this time, it would be conducted in a measured and non-erratic manner. He felt empowered and quietly confident now. He would face him as his equal and look him straight in the eye. Actually, he would face him as his superior; although Miles had heard his mother's declaration that Craig had admitted what he did was wrong and that it wouldn't be repeated, he had, nonetheless, hit his mother. There was no going back as far as Miles was concerned. Containment was the best that could be hoped for. He'd never grow to like Craig, but, for the sake of his mother, he would make an effort to reach some sort of an accommodation. He owed her that much.

He looked back over what had been an incredible and life-changing few weeks. He decided that he needed a holiday.

I upset not only people older than me, but people far more dangerous. I've changed now. There's no going back. That lonely, frightened boy on the train is gone. He doesn't exist anymore. Well, he does in part, but, overall, he's been replaced with a more confident model. I'll really miss the lads. Their involvement with me has been mint. They helped bring out what was inside me. I owe them so much and I'll miss them so much. I miss them already. I'll have to get over and see them, but not for a while. I need to process all that's gone on. A few weeks, but a lifetime ago. So much has happened in such a short time. It's incredible and it's gone ridiculously fast. I'm still spinning. I'll look forward to getting off this particular roller coaster!

Going back's going to be weird, but I'm looking forward to finally lying a lot of things to rest. I'll do that. I need to do it. I'll do it, then I'll go away.

For years, he had dreamt of coming to the Big Smoke, the main place. This was, indeed, the place where he'd earned his spurs and where he'd made his mark. He had also realised that London certainly contained its fair share of ponces, wideboys and crime bosses; regrettably, though, he hadn't seen any slags. He'd certainly lost his innocence, though not in the way he'd hoped. If asked had he seen any action whilst in London, he would, of course, lie. He had to, really. Everyone else would. He had also realised that it was dirty, vile, cheap, disposable, dishonourable, harsh, angry and very unforgiving. He'd seen a lot in his short time there; too much for someone so young.

However, now, here he was, on his way back to Carlisle. For years, he had wanted to leave Carlisle. Carlisle was everything London wasn't. It was small, accessible, familiar, slow, parochial, friendly and laidback. It housed its fair share of petty criminals, rumour mongers, gossips and small town bruisers. Miles, however, didn't have to worry himself with such mere details. He had rendered Baskin impotent, his mum still loved him, and not only did he have Jez in his corner, he now had Beanmonkey, too.

The train was now approaching the platform. He gathered his thoughts together. He looked around at this magnificent, iconic of London termini. He patted the side of the train and stepped up inside. He was now ready to revisit his old world.

Index of Slang

Page 13 – Bollox – Noun 1 the testicles. 2. Rubbish, nonsense. Reverse usuage "The Bollox" meaning brilliant, great, fantastic.

Page 20 – Ponce – Noun 1. A contemptible person. 2. An effeminate male. 3. An ostentatious male. Verb. To beg or freeload

Page 23 – Haway – Northern English expression when mixed with let's get gan meaning to hasten departure. Haway lets get Gan – let's go.

Page 28 – Shagger – Verb. To copulate, to have sex

Page 33 – Adj. Good, nice, pleasant. E.g."She was a **canny** lass

Page 40 – bang out – meaning unjust

Page 48 – grass – Noun - someone who through deception gathers information and subsequently passes it on to the authorities.

Page 83 – Twatting – Verb. To hit, to thump. E.g."I twatted him before he had chance to **twat** me"

Page 107 – Chavvie – Noun – A person usually of poorly educated working class origin who dresses casually in designer sports clothes and vulgar jewellery.

Page 150 – Rozzers – Noun. A policeman/woman

Page 160 – Scroat – Noun. 1. A contemptible person. 2. An abb. of scrotum. 3. A young criminal.

About the Author

Derek Walsh read humanities at the University of Bedfordshire and it was during this time that he was infected with the ambition to be a writer. Before embarking upon novel writing, he was involved in music and penned a few songs which he performed in two rock/indie bands.

The human condition, the richness and diversity of life and a love of words inspire Derek to write. He is struck by the absurdity and the contradictions that lie beneath most given scenarios and enjoy bringing them to the fore through my writing.

Derek Walsh currently lives in the town of Reading in the south of England.

CPSIA information can be obtained at www.ICGtesting.com
Printed in the USA
BVOW041020241011
274391BV00020B/1/P